Safe in Your Head

"Furniture" was published in *Glimmer Train* as winner of the Family Matters contest.

"Suffer The Children" was published in a slightly longer memoir form as "These Innocent Lambs" in *Creative Nonfiction: Our Roots Are Deep With Passion*.

"Nonna" was published in the *Adirondack Review*.

"Ghost Story" was published in *Night Train*.

"Shot" was published in *Night Train Firebox Fiction*.

"Cold War" was published in *Waccamaw Journal*.

"The Things We Own Make Us Safe" was published in *Patterson Literary Review*.

"A Kiss for Heaven's Sake" is forthcoming in *Italian Americana*.

"Bad Luck" is forthcoming in *Voices in Italian Americana. (V.I.A)* and was an Honorable Mention in Glimmer Train's Fiction Open and in New Letters Fiction Prize.

Safe in Your Head

A Novel in Stories

Laura Valeri

STEPHEN F. AUSTIN STATE UNIVERSITY PRESS
NACOGDOCHES ★ TEXAS

This book is a work of fiction. The characters, incidents,
and dialog are drawn from the author's imagination or used
fictitiously and are not to be construed as real. Any resemblance
to actual events or persons, living or dead, is coincidental.

SAFE IN YOUR HEAD

For information, address
Stephen F. Austin State University Press
PO Box 13007, SFA Station,
Nacogcohes TX. 75962.
sfasu.edu/sfapress
sfapress@sfasu.edu

Distributed by Texas A&M University Press Consortium
tamupress.com

First Edition: May 2013
978-1-62288-011-9

1. Fiction 2. Short Stories

CONTENTS

For Nello

Furniture

I

Babbo said everything was bigger in America. He said it so often that the kids bounced on their thighs all through the plane ride, thinking about America's big buildings, big cars, and big burgers. To them, even the plane ride was eventful, with tin foil mini-packages of roasted peanuts and coloring books with crayons. Their legs were cramped and their eyes heavy with lack of sleep, but the kids didn't want sleep. They looked out the airplane window at the clouds and called out the shape of warriors, of ancient Indian leaders, of horses and dragons, and of bears staggering towards huge banana trees.

Their father worried about practical matters: finding the luggage, which was heavy and not always well packed, like the one suitcase that he'd discovered was not locking right and had to secure with a piece of twine. Babbo was not in the habit of buying things new. Things old had a use until they had no use anymore, but he knew that use could be gotten out of a thing much more than most people realized. If a lock was broken on a suitcase, it could be repaired. And if it could not be repaired, it could be rigged with another lock, or with some duct tape or twine. Why throw away a perfectly good suitcase? He had enough money to buy a new one, true, but if there was anything Babbo had learned in ten years of being the manager of a pharmaceutical company was that wastage was wastage, no matter what else you called it. If a suitcase still preserved most of its use, then a little broken lock was no reason to waste money on a new one. That is how companies worked, and that is how family finances should be managed.

It was September 1979, the Pope had died, and a new one had been selected, and this, to Mamma, indicated time for change; it was a sign of things to come, hopeful things, things with sacral direction. Although Mamma despised Babbo's habit of preserving every last piece of furniture, book, scrap, cloth or junk, for the most part she went along with what he said because, after all, pover'uomo, he was a provider, a good one at that. Sometimes, though, Mamma would get tired of the same old furniture with the same old scuff-marks and scratches, and all the things that didn't match, like an old leather recliner and a classic buffet, and an arched overhead lamp from the sixties. If Mamma wanted new furniture, she'd have to endure days of screaming back and forth, the naming of mutual flaws, "Because you're cheap," she would say, or sometimes, "Because you have the taste of a farmer."

The kids would pick up on these recurring phrases and bounce them at the dinner table, volleying them back and forth: "Because Babbo is cheap!" the boy declared, a fork raised to the sky, a piece of spaghetti on his shirt, and the girls, already snorting sauce out of their noses, ducked their heads and covered their mouths, glancing at Babbo, who was eyeing Mamma with a watery look to show how much a father has to endure out of love: "Do you see? It is your fault they don't respect me." Of course, to Babbo respect meant obedience, but sometimes it just meant respect; it meant being able to enjoy a meal at the table without his only son raising a fork at him to call him cheap.

Babbo filled out immigration forms for the whole family. The plane was bouncing over clouds and air pockets, and America was nearing closer, Italy pulling farther away, with it all its high taxes and its strangling bureaucracy, so difficult there to make do with a bourgeoisie life style. Babbo was meant for the kind of money and style only seen in America. He'd worked twelve years for his boss, a viscount who never had to work for anything himself; Babbo worked hard to put the Italian firm on a map, he the son of a small town pharmacist, and the grandson of a Jew whose relatives had been shipped off to Auschwitz during Mussolini's madness. Now he was coming to America, like the romance of war songs:

Mamma mia dammi cento lire
che in America voglio andar

So he had escaped from Milano, its smell and its second-place-ness to metropolises like Paris and New York something that he gladly left behind.

The kids finally fell asleep. They dreamt of leaping frogs, singing lizards and gigantic burgers. Mamma was dreaming of furniture.

Long lines at Immigration. A confusion of luggage and artificial lights. Humorless officers stamping and checking forms. Babbo rushed to the conveyers and pulled off the heavier pieces with the help of the boy, and the girls who were tired and jetlagged followed his orders: "Find us a cart. Put that one on top. Hold this." Babbo was full of commands.

Then there had been the business of finding a cab and all the huff of traveling. The kids sat in the back for their very first ride to New York City; they pointed at the cars that passed them on the highway. There were minivans and sedans and trucks, some so large as to look obscene. Traffic lights hung by wires and swung with the wind. The boy spotted a stretch limo as the girls looked distracted:

"That one. That one is the biggest so far," he said.

"That's a limousine," said the oldest girl. She yawned and stretched and then she declared that a limousine didn't count. They had those in Italy, too.

After the furniture from Milano arrived at the port all boxed up in steel containers, Babbo showed the girls and Mamma around the city. "Look kids. Look at these tall buildings." He pointed at the skyscrapers, which had names, and sometimes, stories to go along with them. "That's the PanAm Building. It once had a helicopter on the roof, but one day there was an accident and the helicopter killed people on the street, so now there is no more helicopter. In America the lawyers have so much power, and the people like to sue so much that a helicopter like that, killing people, will put a stop to things at once. That building is the Waldorf Astoria, the most famous hotel in the whole world. That one over there is the Chrysler Building."

The girls looked up at their Babbo's finger and followed the stories. They wore white tights and wool skirts and coats that rubbed against their calves and made their legs itch. They wore flat, black patent shoes that were too delicate for the city's pavement. The soles had worn thin from so much walking; they could feel the things they stepped on with their toes. The girls were tired. There was dirt on the building facades, windows boarded up with plywood and tape, buildings so old they ought not to be standing. Broken cigarette boxes stuck to the sidewalk that people kicked or flattened with their thick-soled shoes; candy wrappers floated and bobbed in puddles of black water that had gathered in potholes from the rain. Plastic bags clung to poles, slamming with the wind against a thigh, a calf, a car's bumper, fluttering for a moment or two, before slapping an arm and spraying a pant leg with dirty rain water. Bodies all over New York, walking fast and quietly, no one looking at anyone else. What the girls noticed the most was that in these great crowds few were talking.

Babbo hustled the children along. "Come on," he waved. He did not want the kids to talk to the homeless man in the tattered winter coat who smelled like moldy cheese and bad wine. The bum unfolded petals of blackened fingers and offered them up to the girls. The girls looked, their pink mouths sucking in cold wind and stink. "Don't look at those men," Mamma warned. She pointed to the display windows of Fifth Avenue, the Gucci furs, the Tiffany jewelry, the glamour-stained hallway of the Waldorf, with its large chandeliers and expansive carpets. "Look at the furniture," Mamma said. When they were out in the cold again, Babbo looked up at the skyscrapers. "Isn't it great?" Babbo's eyes were wet. "Kids, this is the capital of the world. You are in the center of the world."

They ate their first meal out at Zoom Zoom, so that Babbo could demonstrate the ingenuity of fast foods. He ordered hot dogs, loaded with mustard and sauerkraut and some green stuff even Babbo could not pronounce in English. He offered the hot dog to the girls, but the girls smelled mustard and turned their faces away, covering their noses. Babbo ate the hot dog and the girls ordered burgers. These, too, looked nothing like the burgers sold in Italy, frozen patties that Mamma bought in a box and fried in a pan with olive oil. Those patties tasted good, but not so very much like beef.

"This is real meat," Babbo said, weighing the American burger in his open palm. "Not like those spam patties back home."

Babbo had a funny name for the milk they drank in Italy, too. By comparison to the milk in America, the Italian milk tasted like the piss of an angry cow.

The boy made a jolly face when they ate dinner at night, a mug of warm milk to accompany his meal.

"Nothing like a good swig of the piss-of-an-angry-cow," he declared, brandishing his mug like a Viking's horn, and taking a good swig that would leave a thick and warm milk mustache on his upper lip. Sometimes he said it when the girls were drinking, so that one of them would start to cough, and the other would snort milk out her nose, and Mamma would look horrified as milk dribbled on a pajama top or a terrycloth robe.

She whined, "Oh nohhh," with her mouth twisting against those things that reminded her of a farmer's way. So far she had come from the small town on the water where she was born, a quiet village of cobbled streets and fisheries. And now her own children acted with the manners of peasants, and her husband with the taste of a farmer, and they were holed up for days in this hotel! So far she had traveled to come so near to nowhere at all.

The girls were not used to the pickles and the ketchup and the mayonnaise on the fast food burgers, and so their first few weeks, instead of eating dinner with their Babbo and Mamma and their brother Luca in the kitchen of the hotel suite, they laid with their stomachs in knots on their Big American Hotel bed, writing letters to their girlfriends in Italy, using paper so thin it was like the papers that butchers used in Italy to separate slices of prosciutto. They felt amused that airmail paper was like crinkled silk, so fragile that you had to be careful to cross out a word or you might scratch a hole right through it. On this very thin paper, they tried to write about how it felt to look outside their window and see only a dirty brick wall, how the windows would open only a little crack, how even the shops had thick iron bars, and everything was so dirty, and bread tasted limp, and tomato sauce was sweet like ketchup, and it was hard to shop for anything when store managers followed them around the store and cashier ladies shut their lips tight when they spoke Italian, but instead they ended up describing only the size of American cars. They asked their friends about the gossip back in Italy. All the disparate friends, which before would not speak to each other, now teamed up together, writing hurtful things: "Since you've left, Giuliana has become my best friend..." and other small betrayals that are impossible to articulate on paper thin and flimsy like a best friend's loyalty.

The girls rode the metro bus to Italian school and kept their pass in a conference tag sleeve that belonged to their Babbo. The first time on the bus the driver had barked at them in American, his voice full of something rich and sure, something condemning and authoritative at once. The girls leaned forward, crouching, asking "So sorry?" and "Excuse me?" even as people pressed impatiently against them, wanting to squeeze in. They felt defeated by the mystery of the bus driver's commands. He waved to the contraption near his seat, a money counter which clicked and ticked restlessly even with no coins in its clear plastic top. Someone stepped forward and gave them each quarters to drop in the ticking machine, sighing with the weight of a reluctant favor, and the bus driver waved them in. The girls sat far to the end, smears of shame burning their forehead and cheeks. They breathed into the tops of their wool coats, their chin crowding their swallowed breaths. Kind people tried to explain, the same rich tones coming out of their mouths, the same bitter coffee of sounds.

"Where are you from?" they asked.

"Italy," the girls said. That was as far as kindness got them.

The people nodded, women with grey flecked hair hugging grocery bags, a business man in a blue, gray, black raincoat holding briefcase on his lap scratched his mustache. People with eager smiles offering good will like spare change. The girls wanted to tell these kind people something, but it all turned an awkward jumble of "hummm" and "aaaaah," each missing word another notch and dent on their armor of vanity. What was the price of thinking themselves able to ride a bus, for thinking themselves capable of understanding passes and bus routes, for being betrayed by what they thought they knew? The price was a quarter, a quarter each.

II

The apartment they rented was in German Town, a big building complex with a cobbled street closed to traffic (a luxury in New York, had said the real estate agent) and an elaborate playground where the girls spent more time than they should have talking to boys in street clothes, in dirty t-shirts and ripped pants, boys who glided around on skateboards, boys who barreled into people when they failed one of their air stunts and never apologized, their mouths turned away, their mutters lost to the wind or to the rumble of their skating contraptions.

It was 1980 and Babbo told the girls they were not allowed to talk to those boys.

"But why?"

There was no why, only that they could not: because they were girls, and that was that, and if they insisted, Babbo said, "Because, insomma, I am your father, and you must obey me."

The girls rolled their eyes and crossed their arms over their chest and made a big show of huffing and puffing. Babbo then bought a membership to the condo's health club, which had a swimming pool, and a sauna, and an exercise room with free weights and machines. Every night when Babbo came back from work, he demanded a report from the girls: had they gone to the health club? And how long had they spent in the pool? Did they use the sauna, too? And the exercise room? Was it crowded? Which machines did they use? How warm was the water in the pool?

If they said they didn't use the sauna, or the exercise room, or if they could not remember the temperature of the water in the pool, he'd asked them why they could not remember. Of course, it didn't matter why, only that they had to think about it, and depending if they bit their lips, or rolled their eyes, or sighed real deep before answering, he knew how long they'd been there, or even if they'd been there at all. He reminded them that the club cost good money, good *hard-earned* money, and they should know he wasn't the Swiss Bank, and they should use the club, and not only the pool, but the sauna and the exercise room, too, because it had cost him money and, Per Dio!, it had to be worth it!

The girls rolled their eyes, and lately they had taken to making some comment in the American way, some purr of slang that he could never quite catch but that he was sure was disrespectful. So he raised the pitch of his voice, "What was that? What did you say to your Babbo?" And it didn't matter if they clarified or not because he still didn't understand it. So instead he'd just slap the top of their heads, not hard enough to hurt, but hard enough to ruffle up their ponytails, and to remind them of where they came from. "Bada bene." Mind yourself.

In the beginning, Mamma thought that she might celebrate the start of the new decade by driving a new car. It had been fun to pick a big one, with space in the back (enough to carry a couch in it) that Americans called Station Wagon. It made her think of cowboys, the car, of women in large bonnets and long skirts traveling through billowing dust across deserts, with boxes and kids piled up in the back, and cows and mules following behind. But the traffic in New York was thick, a blast of horns, almost constant, fraying her nerves, and noxious exhausts seeping in through the vent and giving her migraines. There were rules to the parking, too, more elaborate than the Italian tax system: sometimes on this side of the street, sometimes on the other, and they had to get up at four or five, the streets all muddy and wet, to go move the car one way or the other.

But Mamma surprised the kids at school, loaded them up in the back of the wagon and brought them sealed snack packs of lupini beans that she had found at a gourmet deli in midtown.

"Lupini!" the girls cried nostalgically, biting the skin off the beans with their front teeth and sucking at the soft yellow meat with their pink tongues.

Mamma watched her girls in the rearview mirrors and noticed their faces had lost their softness, cheekbones pushing at the edges, pulling their skin tight. Soon Mamma was lost in this gridmaze of buildings, which all looked the same from corner to corner. She stopped at a gas station, her English tentative, and waited for the pudgy-faced, pimpled American in the baseball cap to help her out. They were so helpful, these American boys, calling her "ma'am" and smiling their blue-eyed smile, even when she could not distill a word of meaning out of the spill of their greetings. The gas attendant boy was leaning helpfully towards her as she rolled down the window and folded her pinky and ring finger, wishing for a moment that this would be enough for him to understand. But he only smiled and repeated his fluid greeting, and so she thrust her hand out again and said: "Excuse me. Where is turd avenue?"

"Ma'am?"

"Turd." She held up the three fingers. "Turd Avenue."

There was an explosion of laughter in the wagon, the kids hissing half words to mock her. The gas attendant poked his head in, looking at the girls in the back, at the boy in the front.

"Stop it. Stop it, now, c'mooooon." She said it in English for the sake of the gas attendant because she could not bear being rude to a poor fellow like this one, working at a gas station, his shirt so white and his pants smeared with grease. (What little money his parents must have had to send a teenager to work!) She knew people like this very well, her father a steel-mill worker, her mother a farmer's daughter and a supermarket checkout girl, simple people who knew dignity and hard work. She tapped at the gas gauge, wanting to apologize for this bouquet of shame in her wagon, her three uneducated kids, laughing disrespectfully in front of a stranger.

"So sorry," she said, opening her mouth wide to simulate the proper enunciation. "I need foil! Foil, please."

"Ma'am?"

Her youngest, the boy, laughed so hard he was hissing now. He laughed open mouthed, looking at her with tears in his eyes, yawning silent words with his big mouth of laugh. He was trying to tell her something, and the American gas attendant shifting on his feet, looking at him like someone expecting to be robbed, said, "What do you want, Lady? What's going on here?"

"So sorry..." she pleaded with her deformed English.

"So sorry," mocked her son, his vowels large, and his face foolish-looking, as though she were an idiot child just learning to speak. She slapped her boy over the head, but he laughed even harder then, raising his arm to protect his face and, still laughing, saying, "What are you hitting me for?" sounding so American it broke her heart. The girls in the back laughed, too, one grabbing the front seat and saying, finally, like it was a great effort, "She wants fuel. That's what she means. She means fuel."

"Fuel, that's what I said," she insisted, but the American gas attendant had lost all of that wholesome good cheer to his face. He turned his back on her and said something that she could not grasp, something that ended with "your kind" although there was nothing kind in the way he said it, nor in his "ma'am," or in his blue eyes.

III

Babbo calls her *the old hag*, but there is a cynical smile pulling at the corner of his mouth when he describes her, a glint in his eyes that speaks of admiration, of *his* America, the thing he flew three thousand miles to be a part of. Her name is Dorothy, and she is on the ice rink every Saturday, so reliable that even Babbo has learned her name, so many people talking about her. To Babbo, Dorothy is a spectacle of American strangeness, like the hotdogs and sauerkraut his daughters will not eat. Dorothy is now maybe eighty years old, but she is there, every Sunday, on that lake frozen over with winter. The snow on the pines and spruces attenuate the sounds of kids who fly around her on the ice, on hockey skates, their hands fisted against the cold, and their scarves flying behind them. Dorothy is dainty, a figurine of pink chenille floating slowly over the silver blue. Now and then she lifts a tremulous leg behind her, a smile stubbornly pulling on her taut, papery face. She is crepe silk and tulle, beautiful from a distance, only her slowness betraying her age: as old as the bisnonno they have left back in Italy, his cardigan always soiled with buttery pasta and flecks of pipe tobacco, his ears enormous but too old to capture words. Dorothy is as old as that, maybe older.

The snow falls thickly now. The fog stretches its flaky condensation low to the ground. Dorothy looks like a ballerina dancing languidly through veils. She moves without a spared gesture, grace battling against the tremors of her legs and arms. She is fragile, and when she holds still, her breath a flutter of steam rising upwards, she reminds the girls of the flat, plastic ballerinas they would stick on old Styrofoam disks for packing cakes back at home: perpetually en point, their pink painted toes lifting at the end of a rigid flat leg. Dorothy spins awkwardly, her hands poised like opened lilies, her smile reaching back as if to better days.

"Look at that shameless old woman, all fluffed up like a show-room poodle! Look at her all dressed up in a doll's outfit," Babbo says. Still, his voice pitches high as he laughs, and the girls can detect a hitch in his sureness, a bow to her courage, to her lack of self-awareness.

Babbo mocks it, but watching the old lady, he knows exactly what he lacks in America. At work, the secretaries have recently pooled together to write petitions to the human resources department complaining that his smell is offensive. What Dorothy has is the Americanness that feels just beyond his grasp. In Italy, secretaries would have been too afraid of him to complain about the overtime work he gave them, let alone about his smell. They would not forget that their salary and their company's standing rested on his stinking foreigner's shoulders. Mamma presses his clothes, dry-cleans his shirts. He showers dutifully, every time after a soccer game, and at least twice per week. Babbo cannot smell anything on himself but loyalty and hard work.

The snowflakes fall softly now on Dorothy's blonde hair, tufts of it glimmering like cotton candy over the comb of her tiara. The girls blow into their cold hands and let their breath condense around their reddened noses. And maybe because of the thought of the plastic ballerinas at nonna's house, the youngest of the girls is briefly back home, in a minivan that used to pull up to the school in Milan by the front gates of their small condo complex. The van had carried her home from school only maybe three times, such few times that to remember even one of those times is surprising. It was a failed attempt of the school to provide transportation for children, an American thing that died for having no strong legs to stand on, like Dorothy, only an echo of something. But the memory manages to be found. She fondles this memory a moment, a few seconds' worth, no more. The kids on the bus are passing around a pack of chips. She puts one in her mouth, salty and satisfying. She puts another in her mouth before returning the sack to the boy who shared it with her and says: "It's true you cannot have just one." She is repeating a commercial that plays incessantly on television after the eight o'clock Carosello cartoon show. It occurs to her now that this commercial was stolen from American television, culled by an expatriate Italian from the endless reels of advertising that interrupt too frequently even the news on tv. And though it is a dull and boring idea, it carries with it other smells and images, like catching a quick drink from the spigot in the condo's yard after playing tag, the water smelling of chlorine and moss splashing on her chin and shirt top. And after that she sees the soft glow of the bakeries in Corso Lodi, early in the morning when it is still foggy and grey, the sweet smell of onion focaccia sold by the square softening the dreariness of a school day, making her hungry for a piece of her land. She even misses the cartine geografiche Italiane, maps of Italy rolled up in sheets and sold to third graders for a few hundred liras for geography classes, glossy and bright with pastel orange and azure. These things that she never thought important invade her now with pungent obsession, claiming her like the voices of Ulysses' sirens. And she cannot help but mourn for the many tiny shards of her past life that will become American counterfeits, for all the things she will trade or part with in order to adapt and belong, already seeing the life ahead of her stretch out like Dorothy's hands.

On the lake, Dorothy answers with a pose, her chin lifted, her forehead collecting snowflakes that will melt their crystalline shape between eyebrows and wrinkles. Babbo, now hunched over the iron railings, has lost his snide jokes. The muffled sounds of happy skaters come at the family as if from a great distance. Babbo gazes past Dorothy at the thickened tree clusters behind the lake, reaching to each other against the backdrop of a grey New York skyline. The treetops, huddled together, seem to be sharing a dirty secret, a thing of the future traded with the wind. Mamma lovingly rubs Babbo's back, as if Dorothy's stillness has brought them both something. A glimpse of their own courage, maybe; a shaky thing dressed up in showy clothes.

Onion Schiaccia with Rosemary

In spite of its international popularity, you have not tasted how delicious focaccia can be until you've eaten it in Tuscany, where it is known as schiaccia or schiacciata (both words meaning "flattened). Because Italy was separated into independent states until the early 1800's, each region has its own names for popular dishes and breads, which each region prepares according to its own traditions. In Tuscany, schiaccia is eaten for breakfast: commonly baked in a brick oven, it is thin, salty, and much crispier than the other variations. You must rise early to go to the baker because by eight o'clock, many of the best bakeries will have already run out.

250g water at body temperature
500g type 00 flour
1 package yeast
1 tbsp olive oil
1 teaspoon ground himalayan salt
1 tbsp honey
½ red onion, thinly sliced
2 tbsp finely chopped rosemary leaves
½ tbsp fresh oregano leaves
extra virgin olive oil
fleur de sel

Preheat oven to 500 degrees.

Place flour, water, olive oil, pink salt, and honey in a mixing bowl fitted with a dough hook. Mix at speed 2 for about 5 minutes. Add yeast. Mix again for another 5 minutes until dough is smooth and silky, neither wet nor dry. Form into a ball and moisten with olive oil. Let rise in bowl under a wet towel for an hour in a warm place .

Pour dough out onto an oiled baking pan. Roughly shape into a rectangle and flatten with a rolling pin till it is about ¼ inch thick. Cover lightly with saran wrap and let rise again, about 2 hours. Prick dough all over with a fork, brush with olive oil, scatter onions, rosemary, and oregano over dough, then lightly sprinkle with fleur de sel.

Bake at 500 degrees for 10-15 minutes till well browned. Remove from oven and let cool. Serve with olive oil and grated Reggiano parmesan cheese.

Remedy for good luck in a new endeavor:

On a dewy morning, gather some fresh flowers, tie them up in a bouquet, then find a road or a path not too far from home that you haven't yet trodden. Leave the bouquet at the intersection, with the flowers pointing towards home. Within the year you will receive a fresh, pleasant surprise.

Ghost Story

I dreamt my mother last night. She was dressed in sack, with her hair iron silver, and she complained again to me.

"Bring flowers to my grave. Roses. Once in a while, you could have a mass said for me. It wasn't so long ago I died."

She wore her knit wool shawl, like she did in the last days of her life, you know, with those petals crocheted into the pattern. It took me hours to do it. When we were young, my mother took care that we learned a trade. My sister learned tailoring, and I learned crochet. I remember crocheting those flowers into the quilts I gave your mother for her wedding, too, and the party favors, oh, you should have seen your mother's wedding's party favors, with the frosted almonds and the silk ribbon tying them together. I did all those roses, one by one, with the petals folded in like they were buds, with pale green and pink cotton threads woven in with the silk. Would you believe it? They were so pretty some of the guests didn't know that they could take them home. They asked us about it: how pretty, these party favors. What are they for?

Anyway, as I was telling you, when I woke up, I had a bad feeling about the dream. The dead don't come talking to you just to complain about the weather. I never dream about my mother. When I do, it's usually because something is about to happen. So anyway, just in case, as soon as I woke up, I had my coffee, and I put on my dress, and I called your cousin Stefano, and I had him drive me to the cemetery. While I was there, I brought fresh flowers, too, roses like she asked me, because you never know. I brought flowers for the whole family. And it was a good thing that I did, too because your grandfather's grave needed a little dusting and your great grandfather's grave hadn't been visited since your aunt cheated me out of the apartment. And this is the strange part about it. I found the crypt, where my mother's ashes are buried, with the marker split in half with a crack in the stone right by where the rose buds are carved into the tile. And even stranger than that, the vase had been tipped: it had fresh water in it, and someone had put a rose in it already. It was a fresh rose, so it had to be just no more than a few days that it was there, red like blood, the outer petals still a little wet with dew. Who put it there?

I called your aunt, and she said, "Really! I dreamt about mother, too. There was thunder in the dream. I was going to go to the cemetery myself, but my foot is swollen again today."

Thunder! I couldn't help thinking of that cracked stone. In the name of the Father and the Son and the Holy Spirit, I hope it doesn't mean something bad. Oh, Madonnina, it wouldn't be some kind of warning? Anyway, it wasn't your aunt who put the flower there. It wasn't Stefano either. He drove me and he would have told me. I asked Stefano: "It wouldn't be your wife who put the flower there, could it be?"

Cara mia, I don't know why I asked him. His wife is a Communist, don't you know. She doesn't believe in Christ, nor Mary, nor even in the Holy Ghost if it visited her in the bathtub. Besides that, she's as selfish as a Pisano tax collector. I don't think she's visited her own father's grave once since he died three years ago, why do I tell you? But I asked, just to be polite, and of course as expected, Stefano said she hadn't left the house in weeks, on account of some kind of proposal she was preparing for the mayor of Piombino.

So I called just about everyone when I got home. I didn't even take off my coat. Look at it. It's still hanging in the stanzino. You can still see the cold dew on it: just now I got home. Look: my hair is still a little wet with the cold. I called your aunt Bice, and she asked her mother, and I called Giuseppa, and I called Beppina, and Minello, and even Pippo, whom I haven't talked to in years. Nobody had put the rose there.

Déh! It's a mystery.

A red rose, freshly budding, with its outer petals a little bruised, like someone had touched it, plucked the outer petals for luck. A secret admirer, maybe.

It makes me think about the last days when my mother was sick, the dreams she had about a ballerina. You know, in those last days, she was practically incoherent. She couldn't recognize your mother when she came to visit her. She was mostly always sleeping, you know, smelling of saliva and urine, the medicine knocking her out, the bed pan always swishing around a little under the covers before we could get it out. But sometimes she woke up startled from her nightmares, with her hand, bony and withered like a bird's claw, clutching her bosoms with the folds of her nightgown. She wore that shawl then, too, yellowing at the seam, the roses I knitted into it curling at the edges from age and too many washes.

"The ballerina, the poor ballerina!"

She was always ranting on about some ballet dancer she saw in her dreams, a dancer who was threatened by a man in a dark coat and fedora. It was a recurring dream, we thought: she watched a beautiful ballerina perform, and then, always, like the persistence of old age, a man would come to abuse her.

"That dark man! That awful, awful dark man hits her. He takes her arm and twists it until it cracks."

Madonnina, it makes me want to cross myself. Even now I can hear her, that gravelly voice dissolving like the Host with a little bit of spit. *Déh*! We thought it was the hallucinations of near death.

Even your mother once asked me, "Was grandma a ballet dancer before she met Egisto?" And she wasn't even a little girl anymore, your mother.

Now, I would have laughed had it not been my mother's death-bed. A ballerina! We didn't have a penny in the family. We were farmers, all of us, my cousins, my grandfather, all of us but Egisto, whom, as you know, worked in the factory. And before the factory, he worked in the stables, stacking hay and cleaning horse manure. Not that it's something to be ashamed of. The poor have dignity. *Déh!* Even Jesus said it is easier for a camel to pass through a needle's eye than for a rich man to enter Heaven.

Although, now that I think of it, my great grandmother was a countess, yes, and we were always told as children that she once had estates, stables, and wineries, and an olive grove, and a mansion with fireplaces in every room, somewhere up near Grosseto. Hers was a Napolenoic title, and it could be inherited only through male heirs. Nonna Giulia was the only child, so the title died with her, but she did have that title, and the pension of a countess that came with that title, and lands, and all those fine things. You know we are poor as dirt. My mother's father was a farmer. I don't think they had ballet school up in the hills. Because the countess, in addition to the stables and the horses, also had a husband who gambled. He drank, too. And he wasn't above raising a fist to her mouth if she complained about it. The poor woman! She had seven children from that man, and she loved him, loved him loved him, but she lost her teeth on that love. She was all drenched up in his love like a rag to wash floors is drenched up in dirty water. She was all torn up about it. And he drank and gambled away the stables, the winery, the grove, square kilometer by square kilometer. All their savings, her jewels, even her dresses, shoved over the wood boards of a tavern table, handed over to the money lenders together with the dirt under the nails that tended and nurtured every trellis in that olive grove. *Déh!* All that work, exchanged for sweaty playing cards and dice.

In the end, the sons, who had already left, penniless, to raise their own families, went to the house one night. I imagine them still, with those long boots they wore in those days, right up to the knee, the soles all caked up in mud because they were farmers, every last one of them. They waited until he was in a tavern, drinking, what else? And gambling away his wedding band. The sons snuck up the back stairs like thieves and packed up their mother like she was an arse's saddle. She didn't want to leave, though. She was so in love with that man that she kicked and screamed as they hoisted her up on the wagon, a hand on her mouth and an arm wrapped around her flailing arms.

"Mamma!," they said, "If we don't take you with us that man will kill you. He will pummel you to death and sell the teeth in your head for game."

They took her to Follonica, to the farm where my mother grew up. They made her swear that she would never go back to him. But one day she made them take her back to Grosseto. They would not let her get close enough to the house, and by then it wasn't a mansion anymore because he had sold that, too. There was only a crooked thing of a hut that he lived in, full of cracks and holes. They took her, but they would not let her speak to him, only watch him as he sat in front of his poor excuse of a house, with his cards and his wine and his hate of life. Anyway, he already had a mistress, always trying to marry into money, to find some small scrap of silk or gold to gamble away. But my great grandmother wanted to see her husband one last time. She said he was beautiful. She watched him from the edges of the hill, through the olive bushes, like a thief, watched him stooping over his cup, his hair falling down over his cheekbones, watched him until the sky was red and bruised like old love.

"Ah, how beautiful he is," she sighed, with a hand to her bosom and her cheeks flushed like the soprano in an operetta. All the acres of land, the title, the jewels didn't matter one thing to her. It was only for the sons that she left him. But they wouldn't let her near him anymore.

One of her sons, I think it was my grandfather, said, "Mamma, if he raises his fist to your mouth again, I will kill him. Don't make me kill my father." So that was the reason she never went back to him.

And so you see in your family you have a countess. I bet you'd never think it, *Déh!* You're so used to seeing your grandmother with this apron, these slippers, this ugly wool coat and foulard. You'd never think I had some blue blood in me, would you? And to think that to support your mother after my husband died I had to work in the cooperative, twelve hours a day. They'd lock us in the storehouse overnight with the rolls of dry pasta and the sacks of flours to do inventory. Once a mama cat had her litter in there. She had crawled up in a nest of linguine. It was all soaked in cat blood with seven mewing wet pink mouths lifting their cries from the rolls: you'd think it was an American movie, all those wet heads and pink tongues budding up from the rolls of dry linguine like aliens. But no, it was our bad luck, crying to us from the wet womb of misery. We had to pay for the ruined pasta of course, even though it wasn't our fault that the mama cat chose to have her litter in the storehouse. They said it was our fault because we had to take care of vermin. Well so it is. Flushed down like so many other dreams, that countess title your great grandmother lost, and that mama cat, too, with all her screaming kittens. And your grandmother ruining her knees all day in the cooperative. *Déh!* Sometimes you'd think God is a crazy man.

But my mother's dream, now that makes me concerned. I wonder what she meant, coming after all these years, asking for roses. Because, you know, the dead have a way of speaking to us from the grave. When they want to tell us something, they know how to break through from the other world. I only wish they were clear about it. Let me call your cousin Rosalinda. She's good with dreams. Maybe she can help me figure it out. My mother, she was dressed in sack, except for that shawl. That means she's doing penance, poor woman. *Déh!* As if we hadn't paid enough in living that we have some debt left over in death. Ay, mamma. Let me call Rosalinda: she's good with dreams. She can help me figure it out.

Fried Rabbit

Rabbit is a dish typical of the Tuscan region, where the vast majority of the population were farmers. Menus at traditional Tuscan restaurants will offer many variations for this tasty treat.

One whole rabbit, cut into pieces.
Flour for dusting
1 cup milk
2 cups bread crumbs
½ tbsp each dried garlic, oregano, rosemary, and basil
2 cups olive oil
Salt and Pepper

Dredge the rabbit pieces in flour and refrigerate for 1 hour. Add spices to bread crumbs and incorporate well. Dip rabbit in milk, then roll in breadcrumbs till thoroughly coated. Fry in 350 degree oil until browned on the outside and cooked through on the inside. Remove from oil, drain, and season with salt and pepper immediately. Serve hot with roasted potatoes.

Remedy for warding off evil:

When carried in your pocket, a goat foot or hairs from a buck's chin will protect the wearer from evil. Washing your floors and walls with salt and water will keep any spell or evil intentions sent your way from having any effect.

The Things We Own Make Us Safe

It's after school. The TV plays the jolty clips of a riot downtown. It's supposed to be Mazinga time, the Japanese robot cartoon, with Aktarus the hero pilot whose tormented emotional life is the subject of my fantasies. Matteo on the 14th floor has a color tv, and I wish he'd invite me over. But the picture on the black and white screen is not of the youthful Aktarus, with his huge eyes always brimming with emotion, but rather it's the static shot of Aldo Moro, the former Prime Minister, whose fingers are joined together and pressing against his chin rendering his thoughtful face thinned out and worried. Kidnapped, says the reporter: by the Brigate Rosse, which, the television says, are Communist terrorists infiltrating Italy from the Soviet Union. Then the tv shows us cracks like crystal spider webs on the Fiats and Alfas lined along the crowded Piazza Del Duomo. Exploded storefronts. Blood. Smears of spray paint vivid enough to come through even on my black and white tv.

Mamma hisses. Babbo ticks his tongue. They've both been expecting this. Babbo even says, "I knew it!" as though explosions in an elegant mall are like thunderstorms and earthquakes, predicted from charts and weather patterns.

I don't tell them that I'm scared, but at night, already, I keep my shoes close to the bed and a change of clothes under my pillow. An earthquake struck two years ago in 1976, just a few hundred miles north from here. I think of the pulsing of magma deep in the earth, smashing and knocking against the layers of rocks beneath us. I think of bombs, crumbling buildings, tear gas, the twisted up condoms still white with juice and the broken syringes in the abandoned factory behind our condo, and all the things that press against my skin with the darkness when I try to sleep. I jolt as I hear crashing glass coming from outside. Mamma says the factory building behind our apartment building is a drug coven. I hear laughter, a gunshot. I close my eyes, touch my clothes under the pillow, and wish myself asleep.

At school again today the shutters are down in spite of the warm sunshine. The Syndicate declared a strike. Matteo, who used to chase me up the garage ramp when we still had training wheels on our bikes, sees me wandering alone at recess and calls me Big Nose, and his cronies elbow each other, laughing. They circle me, one of them singing, "Valenza, Valenza," and the other one yelling, "Nice scarf! Can I have it?" just as he snatches it. It leaves a burn mark on my neck but I manage to grab an end just before he runs off. He keeps pulling, and I hang on. Each of the boys grabs another piece. I hit them as they get close, and they laugh and edge their way back, until there's three of them hanging from the other end. They spin me as they swing in a wide arc, me at the center, my arms stretched out, my fists clamped tight, and my serious face reflecting their laughter as they run a wide circle around me, using my scarf like the spoke of a wheel.

"The Big Nose is strong!" they brag, until they're bored with me, and I fall on my butt. I have the scarf, but now it's all misshapen. The boys skip around in their long, grey wool coats, knowing they won without winning, and they share the news: "That Valenza girl is some kind of tough. Three of us couldn't take that scarf from her."

The cafeteria workers are already clearing up when I manage to get there, and the kitchen is clanging with pans and silverware.

I pretend not to hear the whispers and the chins nudging in my direction. A siren goes off and all the kids crowd to the window, seeing the Pirelli factory workers cluster around the school's front gates, handling grease-smeared wrenches. From time to time the factory workers come to discuss politics with Principal Gaetani. The teachers pull us away from the windows and tell us to make no sound, Silenzio! Bambini, silenzio! Hold hands, and pray to our Madonna for Signora Gaetani to reason with those men. And we hush, not so much for the warning, but because Gaetani is one round, big-breasted woman with shiny cheeks, looking like a Christmas top in her too-tight suit, and the men in wool hats and gloves with the tips cut off hover over her like seal hunters about to make a kill.

As Gaetani argues with the men outside, her hands jerk in various gestures. Matteo declares: "We should send Valenza out there. She and Gaetani together could beat those guys to a pulp."

There's a girl in our school, Anna Maria. She's pretty, but not so pretty that the older boys from high school will try to take her virginity and then call her a whore. She's nice, but not so nice that she'll be friends with the meridionale girl who speaks only a Sicilian dialect. If someone stole Anna Maria's scarf some blushing boy would champion the miscreants and return it to her with an apology. I fondle my misshapen scarf and a teacher grabs my elbow, hissing: "Valenza, what did you do? The boys told me you beat them up during recess."

On the walls encasing the school gate, someone spray-painted: FASCISTI, ELITISTI MANGIA CANI.

As we roll in for Phys Ed, we notice Mr Rossi has lined the walls of the gymn with monkey bars and nets. Thick hemp ropes hang from the ceiling, some of them knotted up. He's pushing hurdles and a balance beam out of a thickly crammed closet when he notices us gawking and he yells, "What are you all doing there, drooling like donkeys? Go change, *Cretini*."

The first day Mr. Rossi taught P.E. he called us all *cretini,* right off. He said the last guy was fired for being a lazy donkey. As for himself, he was the trainer for the Milan soccer team, and he would show us what athleticism really meant: no snot-taffy whiner on *his* team acting like a donkey! We were all going to be champions. In the middle of this, Guido Neri raises his hand and simultaneously calls out, "That's impossible, Mr. Rossi. I know all the trainers of the Milan. There *never* was a Rossi in the Milan team."

Guido begins a list of coaches, last name first, followed by the years of service to the team; his spindly fingers count all the trainers since 1899. He's being very scientific about it. Mr. Rossi strolls over to Guido's spot on the mattress where he's all curled up and cross legged, and when we least expect it, Rossi swings a hand from behind his back, and Guido's head jerks forward, a crackle of static snapping from his gold curls, and all our laughing immediately recedes inside our lungs and hushes there. This way, Mr. Rossi establishes immediately the kind of teacher he is.

When we girls march in from the change rooms in our shorts, our green sweat pants cast off over our school bags, the boys, already standing on a lineup, stretch their necks to have a good look at us, their skulls too coarse with boy-foolishness to care that Mr Rossi hits them hard enough to make them stumble out of line. A couple of the boys whistle. It's an amateur kind of whistle, full of spit and hiss, and even I can tell by the way the boys snicker that they think that this is what's expected of them. As a respectable Catholic girl, though, I should say something about all this *culo* talk.

"Stop looking at us, *cretino.*"

"Nobody is looking at you, Mazinga," says Matteo, the line of his gaze stopping on my size 40 shoes.

I cross my arms around my waist. Mazinga has square shoulders, gigantic metal legs and a helmet head. Only Alessandra Scaroni is taller than me, and she's looking at me like she's just bested me three turns of jump rope. The cuffs around my sweatshirt reach right above my wrists, and my pants, after only the second wash, rise up above my ankles to reveal the ribbed edge of my tube socks. I'm too tall, even for me.

So, that's why when we are all sitting legs crossed on the mat, waiting for Mr. Rossi to wave our turn to jump on a spring board and flip in the air above a pommel horse, I am startled when our red-faced coach taps me on the shoulder to hand me a blue slip. Without looking at it, I zip it safe into the pocket of my sweat jacket. It's the slip that he gives to the best athletes of the class, the kids deserving to participate in the annual regional Olympics held by the private school system in Milan. It is not the real Olympics of course, but I finger my trophy in the pocket of my sweat jacket.

At dinner, the television is on, and Babbo, in his wife beater, is propped forward as if about to propel himself inside the screen. My brother is laughing over his food. My sister is stuffing bread in her mouth. Mamma says, "Vittoria, that bread will make you fat." Babbo says: "shhhhhh!" He turns up the volume on the television. Another middle class industrialist has been kidnapped. I don't get to share the good news.

This is a common scenario for me these days: I get recruited to play tag, but somebody's grandmother happens by, scowls until I'm forced to look at her, and then as if struck with enlightenment, she shouts, "You're too old to be running around with those kids!" I stand on attention before her wondering what lesson of propriety I missed, when the old woman asks, "How old are you?" When I tell her, the lady hugs her purse and scowls something about my looking old enough to make a baby. I stand there, catching my breath, tempted to look back where my playmates call out already as if from a dream. Never talk back to an old person, says Mamma. The old lady coughs, "Go play," and waves me off without apologies, but by then, I am transformed, a clumsy, long-legged, child-bearing adolescent chasing after little kids.

On the eve of the event, when I can't put it off any longer, I stand in our cramped, blue-tiled kitchen, the table in the corner still crowded with plates, a baguette, and a half-filled water carafe. The television is playing the familiar ditty that announces the day's soccer scores. There, in my pjs and slippers, I proffer evidence of my inclusion in the region-wide olympics: an embroidered school logo that my mother is supposed to stitch onto my too-tight school-issued green sweat jacket.

"By when?"

"By tomorrow."

Mamma says, "Tomorrow I have to take your brother to the doctor."

Babbo lifts off his haunches, slowly, and I see the look on his face when his voice overrides Mom's question about why I waited so long to tell them, and shouts, "Brava!"

The lights of bakeries, grocers and coffee shops glow in the dark of early dawn like candles lit for the dead. Iron shutters groan noisily as they're raised up from the ground with metal hooks, screeching with the start of the workday. My mother pushes me out of the cold into the soothing steam of a well-heated butcher shop.

"So early, signora?" asks a surprised butcher. My mother is blue eyed and petite, graceful, and agile. The first boy who tried to kiss her ended up nursing a concussion from the bottle of perfume my mother broke over his head. The perfume was the boy's gift to her.

"Signore," my mother says importantly, sliding me in front of her. "La bambina has a special day today. She's going to be at the arena for an athletic competition."

The butcher understands what my mother wants and looks me over, nodding, "She's very athletic-looking, for sure."

My mother explains her disappointment for not being able to witness her daughter's moment of triumph, and the butcher offers sympathy, a ritual of Italian social propriety that I anticipate but fail to appreciate. After a spell of nods and pleasantries, the butcher persuades my mother that he can fix a great sandwich for the bambina. He hurries off to a haunch of cured pig that hangs from a hook in the ceiling. "I'll cut the prosciutto fresh for you," he pants and proceeds to fillet the pork with a knife, maybe to impress my mother, or maybe because his slicer has some problem we don't know about. I smell the salt in the air, the cured meat teasing my stomach. By the time we get to the school bus, my mind is glued to the paper bag I carry in my satchel. All I can think of is lunch.

Most of us, Mr Rossi's *cretinis*, are comatose with sleep or motion sickness when we roll off the bus. Even Mr. Rossi looks like he swallowed his whistle with his espresso. There are guns going off, and loud speakers crackling numbers, and people are cheering and shouting, and no matter how much I try, I can't hear what he's saying. Bleachers surround an oval-shaped field, edged off with a chain link fence and sectioned in chalk for different competitions. In the time it takes for Mr. Rossi to execute a few terse commands, I've already been distracted by two short sprints, a new battery of runners pinning numbers to their shirts even as another set of runners crosses the finish line.

I wake up from the spell just in time to hear the coach bark: "Don't drink until you've finished racing, no matter how thirsty you get."

Then he pairs me off with Anna Maria, whose hazel eyes and long thin legs have made her popular since fifth grade. Anna Maria hands me a number printed on an ugly white cloth. "Here," she says. "Pin mine on, and I'll pin yours on."

I follow his pointing finger towards a woman with a clipboard calling out our schools' name. We are ushered through a gate, and then someone tells me to take up the indicated position for a thirty-meter sprint. It's on your marks, get set, and the gun shot. I'm paralyzed for a short fraction, and I'm off.

Then it's over.

So I go to my brown bag, which is where my brain is still glued, and I pop open the Fanta, sweet bubbles splashing my parched throat.

"You drank!" Anna Maria stands with arms akimbo, blocking my sun. She grabs my wrist, pulling me up. The crumbs from my uneaten sandwich fall from my lap.

"The other girl got her period so you have to replace her," she informs me.

I let her pull me through the oval field to the far west end. The soda is swooshing in my stomach as we trot towards the race. Coach Rossi waves me to the far back corner of the race field and hands me a baton, his whistle blowing outrage at me.

I bend to touch the line; the gun goes off. I catch someone's elbow with my ribs and I stumble. Red sand rises in small clouds, kicked up by stomping far ahead of me. I'm alone, running through my sweat, the soda swishing in my belly. My thighs and calves cramp up. My feet stomp clumsily ahead. The racetrack curves and I make the mistake of looking down, where all the lines tangle like crochet patterns. I can't tell which lane I should be in. I think I must have drifted when that elbow hit me. I move over one lane, and I spot Anna Maria squatted and ready, her hand pulled behind her. I slow down just as she sprints ahead. I fold over gasping.

Coach Rossi's whistle drops from his mouth as I approach. His fists on his hips he informs me that my lane wobbling cost the team third place. I open my mouth waiting for words but none come. He squeezes my elbow and says, "Valenza, for once, act like a normal person. Pay attention. Don't you want to *win*?"

I wonder if he does, because he signs me up for another event, the high jump with Anna Maria and Alessandra Scaroni. From the other schools no one looks so threatening as one big bulldog of a girl who is taller than all of us, and uglier than if somebody turned Alessandra's face and mine into clay and molded us together in a boring moment in art class. She walks with her arms slightly raised and glowers from under thin, greasy bangs. Her eyes scan over Anna Maria's and Alessandra's faces, but when she sees me, she sucks in her breath. I wave. Anna Maria pulls my arm down, and barks, "Let's go," and I follow her. We're off to *winning*, I reassure myself.

But Alessandra gets eliminated the first round. She gets up from the mat holding both her breasts with her arm, as if to use her voluptuousness as her alibi. Then it's unbearably hot, and it seems to me that I keep getting called up to do more. I'm not surprised to see kids from our school with their lunches and their sodas: they're here for Anna Maria, calling out her name, and Viva! Viva! The school's honor is at stake. Alessandra gets busy doing for the team what she does best: *that girl (the butch girl) is not our age. Look how tall. She must be at least fifteen, left back a few grades.* The boys throw crushed aluminum cans at the wire fence, making bovine sounds. The butch girl ignores them, her face sculpted into a scowl. Once in a while her eyeballs move inside their sockets as she takes a look at me. She hangs, like a carnival gorilla costume from a perch, her shoulders rounded forward.

I don't know where I am exactly throughout this time. Thinking of my prosciutto sandwich warming up in the sun. Thinking about my Fanta, now probably so overheated that I'll have to shower with it before I manage a sip. Thinking about how Anna Maria just fell on the matt with the iron bar clanging after her, leaving me to defend the honor of the team. I have to make the jump Anna Maria just failed in order to move up to the next round, but I everything around me has the quality of a bad dream. Anna Maria breaks out from the cluster of eliminated competitors and waves for me to wait. When she comes close enough, she clenches her hands into fists. "Show that girl we're not intimidated by her. You're also tall; you're big. We can *win*."

I look over to my nemesis, her acne-scarred cheeks stretching into a strained sort of smirk, and it occurs to me that to our fans on the other side of the chain link fence the only difference between us is our school's logo. But the whistle blows, and I run, and jump, and lift myself up, pulling from gravity as I twist and buck, arching my back high and pulling my legs above me so fast that when I land on the mattress I flip over on my head. Still, the heels of my sneakers brush against the bar and dislodge it.

"Feet!" screams coach Rossi, his hands flying up.

I take my place again, panting. I hear them calling out from the bleachers: "Do it Valenza. Do it." My heart answers with a thu-thump that drowns them out. In my stomach something is boiling, foaming a little as it rolls into a scalding bubble. But I give them what they want. I run and jump and lift and twist and fall and flip and I remember to lift my feet for the honor of Mr. Rossi and the *cretini* of Scuola Europa. A shout charges at me from the bleachers. My schoolmates are on their feet, grabbing and rattling the chain link fence. The butch girl stands up, her eyes webbed with red capillaries.

In spite of the invectives from my teammates, the big girl trots to the white line, her buttocks quivering a bit. She lifts her thick legs, first one and then the other, and she's over the bar just like that. It would be funnier in fast motion, hilarious if the segue wasn't me, drenched in sweat, trying to put another millimeter between the red clay and my feet. I manage to tag her two more rounds before I'm disqualified, a deflated awwww oozing from the crowd when the bar clangs to the ground on my second attempt.

"You tried," mutters coach Rossi, looking at his clipboard as he scribbles down my score. My schoolmates have already abandoned the bleachers to join other events, other games of popularity and success. I sit alone in the shade to savor my lunch.

A carnival sets up in the muddy lot across from the school, and men in colored aprons offer cotton candy, inching their carts close to the gate, accepting liras from the stretched hands of children who sneak their fuzzy prize through the iron bars. Strands of colored sugar float in the wind with the pollen. Fiats bump across the lot. On the brick walls outside the school, someone has spray-painted a red star enclosed by a circle. When I step out of Mom's cinquecento, Anna Maria waves me down, trots by, and drops her satchel at my feet. "Where did you go after the race?" she demands. I puzzle through her question like trying to decode a passage from Latin. Anna Maria rolls her eyes. Her hands land on her hips as soon as she delivers a green plastic jewelry box and a set of polaroids. "You won second place for the high jump and third for the short sprint," she sighs. "I had to take your place on the podium because from a distance, I look like you."

Former Prime Minister Aldo Moro's face overwhelms the black and white screen of the kitchen's tv. Captured in the static photo is his smile, his mouth curved in a small gash of hope, his eyes dreamy and reflecting relief, even though he stands in front of a great banner where the star inside the circle and the words BRIGATE ROSSE are printed in large letters. Moro looks amused, even, as though all that behind him is a harmless prank he's forced to admit to. He was shot in the back last night. They found him face down in the trunk of a car, that humble smile still on his face.

Babbo says, "Italy's a third world country now. This is a revolution." He and my mother confabulate in the kitchen. The words New York, work visa, mamma, carry metallic echoes, bullets of necessity.

As I hear my parents argue, I finger the pictures of Anna Maria honoring my spot on the podium. Strange. The pictures were taken from far enough that the girl in the Scuola Europa uniform could look like me, if you squinted, if you looked at the picture fast. Babbo says in America everything is bigger: cars, buildings, chickens, even people. I wonder if the gorilla girl on the podium would look like any other girl in America.

For a while I keep the photographs under my pillow, with my sweater, my change of socks. I will take these pictures to America. I will show my American friends of the future this gray podium and this shy, smiling girl whose name I don't even know, who looks at the camera, relieved, almost apologetically so. I will point to her, the tallest bambina, surrounded by chain links and iron gates, beyond maligned whispers and threats of syndicate workers, above Communist terrorists, apoplectic coaches, and gossiping *cretinos*, that bulky girl with the red-rimmed eyes whose uncertain hands still hold aloft, in memory and deed, a triumph for the meek.

Prosciutto Panini

100 grams thinly sliced Prosciutto di Parma
2 tbsp olive tapenade (see attached note)
several leaves of arugula
3 thinly sliced tomatoes
½ thinly sliced red onion
1 tbsp fresh chopped basil leaves
3 thin slices of fresh mozzarella
extra virgin olive oil to taste
¼ tspn freshly cracked pepper
3x6" piece of freshly baked focaccia

Slice the focaccia in half. Spread the inside with olive oil. Toast to brown. Spread a layer of tapenade on the bottom slice of focaccia. Fold several slices of Prosciutto on top. Add tomato and onion. Crack some pepper on top. Add a few more folded slices of Prosciutto. Add thinly sliced mozzarella, then basil leaves, then arugula. Place toasted foccacia on top, slice diagonally, and serve with fresh lemonade.

Olive Tapenade

1 ½ cup seedless green olives
1 ½ cup seedless black olives
¼ cup roasted red pepper
2 tbsp olive oil
2 tbsp lemon juice
1 clove garlic
2 anchovy filets
1 tbsp capers
1 tsp fresh thyme leaves
1 tsp fresh basil leaves
½ tsp fresh rosemary
½ tsp cracked black pepper

Put all ingredients in a food processor. Pulse to a coarse paste. Will keep for 2 weeks in the refrigerator.

Remedy to gain physical attractiveness:

To become more physically attractive, one must leave a bucket of water and aromatic herbs outside in the open, at midnight on the summer solstice . Early in the morning of the first day of summer one must bathe with the water. Doing so will make that person become beautiful to others.

Bad Luck

Mara's mother clutches the pendant in the well of her breasts, a golden guardian angel she's had since Communion. Her head is wrapped in the black foulard of mourning. The streets are crowded with whispers and the shuffling of feet, a funeral procession passing beyond the gathered women and men who stare with faces broken with grief. Some step forward to touch her mother's elbow, saying, "We're so sorry, Liliana. He was a good man, Giorgio was."

Mara nods to a woman who cups her chin and offers a face lined with disappointment while saying, "You behave for your mother now. A girl has her reputation, and without a father…"

Another old woman cuts her off, her hand making a sharp gesture. She is wrapped in a black shawl, which she rearranges over her head as she lifts her arms in a gesture Mara understands only with her feelings. There are no bells ringing, but the funeral turns towards the piazza, and Mara sees the men from the mill waiting, removing their wool caps as the hearse arrives, and holding a fist to their temple in salute.

"I am so unlucky," her mother says to no one in particular. "It's bad luck to replace a lost wedding band. I should have told Giorgio not to bother to buy me a new one."

Mara squeezes her mother's hand. Bad luck: black cats, a hat on the table, salt spilled on the floor, an umbrella opened in the house. Mara thinks it's bad luck to grow up without a father, to be born during wartime, to be on the wrong side of strong.

Mara remembers things, not in chronology. It is as if her father was cut loose from time and drifting like trash in the sea, billowing and gleaming with the reflected sunlight, moving further off shore with the currents, tossed and rolled by the crest of a wave. He appears now as a young man she never met, now as a soldier in a uniform. Sometimes he's an older man with a set chin and dark eyebrows. Sometimes he's dressed in a tuxedo, as if emerging from a fantasy of tropical hotels ringing with Cuban jazz.

At five, Mara plays downstairs in the street, close, like her nonna wants her to, near the front portals of the apartment building. Her building is one of the few that hasn't cracked like bread crust with the heat of the bombs. The sound of an army truck rises above the scraping of shovels, above the usual cries of women calling to each other from balconies as they hang laundry and talk about letters from their husbands at the front. A nub of chalk leaves powdery smears on Mara's fingers, tucked in the seam of her white school apron pocket. In school, the teacher said, "The Americans are here. Now we can afford a little leniency."

Mara wastes the gift of leniency on the asphalt, drawing large squares and circles on the cracked bubbles. She jumps with one leg, then two, her shoes hitting the pavement with flat sounds, and she's flipped a full turn when she sees a man with an army backpack slung on his back. He wears a green jacket tied by the sleeves around his waist, a stained wife beater and khaki pants. Where his mouth and chin should be, there's a thick, black beard clinging to his cheekbones and creeping down his neck.

"*Un soldato*," says someone from above. "One of ours?"

The soldier's uniform, all dusty and torn, makes Mara think of rioting in Piazza Bovio, when men crashed store fronts with cudgels; it reminds her of crying women dressed in black and whispering old men chewing on the ends of an unlit pipe, their caps pulled tight down their foreheads, their eyes moving from side to side as if to spot a rabid dog. It reminds her of the corpses she saw bobbing face down in the water once, before her mother took her away to the farm.

The soldier tilts his head towards the voice. He tips the visor of a hat he isn't wearing, then slowly turns to take in his surrounding, readjusting his army bag on his shoulder, his knees bending a little with the effort, and then he looks at Mara again.

He has blue eyes, like hers, but not like a German's; his are the blue of bruises, webbed in violet and dull like grief. In a sweet tenor voice the soldier asks if she's Liliana's child. He speaks to her the way old people sometimes do when reaching for her cheek with fingers like pincers, saying things like, I knew you when you were this small.

"Mara?" His question is hesitant.

She rolls the nub of chalk between her fingers and stares at him. When he speaks her name again she winces, startled by his realness.

"Is your mother home?" His voice is deep, too rich for the hunger tattooed on the bones that poke from his shoulders.

When he steps towards her, she runs into the cool atrium of the lobby, her shoes click-clacking up the clean stone steps, past the bucket still full with water and soap, past the sudsy mop, up and up to the second floor apartment. Her shouts trail after her, mamma, mamma, through the rectangular well of the stairs. She's so small that she must tip on her toes in order to open the front door of the two-room apartment in Piombino, where she's lived with her mamma since the war ended.

"Mamma, there's a soldier downstairs, a man in uniform. Very dirty."

"A soldier? It's Giorgio!" her aunt shouts from the closet where she's soaking laundry in a plastic bucket.

Mara rushes back out to the landing, her hands grasping the balustrade as she tips on her toes and looks down, hoping maybe for the soldier to be gone.

Women pour out of their homes, crowding the landings of

each of the six floors. Heads poke from the balustrade, scowling upside down, asking, "*Chi e', lo conosci? E' nostro? E' uno dei nostri?*"

Her mother comes up from behind, wraps her hands so tight on the balustrade that Mara sees her knuckles turn pale, cries, "*Madonnina*! It's your father." She bends almost in half with one hand holding her stomach like it hurts, and her knees seem to bend unsteadily as she hurries down the stairs. Mara watches her mother embrace the bearded soldier, her face disappearing into the crook of his neck, and the two of them sway like fronds in the breeze, the soldier's fingers kneading her mother's shoulder blades as he rushes urgent whispers into her ear. Mara curls her tongue around the chalk, tastes it without tasting it.

Her aunt breaths thickly from the threshold of the mop closet, "*E' Giorgio! E' lui.*"

Some of the women shake their heads and somberly return to their apartments with their apron pockets empty of hope, while others say, "Ah! At least, the Cateni boy came back alive."

In the thick of war, when the radio crackled with the voice of Mussolini declaring, "*Spezzeremo le reni alla Grecia,*" and Italian troops sailed off to Greece, Mara lived in the country with her grandfather Egisto. At night, the sky was always bloody, and the hills looked like the stooped backs of old factory workers. But at least there was food, a coarse bread made of dark grain that she dipped in a finger of wine to soften. No mills to attract the airplanes, no bombs whistling and walls rumbling day and night like in Piombino, only the hunger to remind her, only the tough crust of the bread that tasted like disappointment, like loneliness and fear.

From that time, she remembers the clucking of two scraggly chickens that roosted in trees. She remembers geese, a watery soup that her nonna slow-cooked all day, the snails that Mara plucked from the long blades of grass growing around the path she walked every morning. And another memory: skipping stones to scare away a thin stray dog, when the ground popped at her feet, turf spraying on her ankles, her clean white socks splattered with a shower of dirt. Pop. Pop. Pop.

"Corri, corri," her nonno, Egisto shouts. He swoops her up in his arms and hurries down the hill, still crying, run, run, as if forgetting that her legs are wrapped around his waist, already, her weight in his arms slowing them down. Behind them, men in uniform load their guns and fire, fear ripping open her chest with the muted popping of their weapons. She hears the click right before the earth explodes again around Egisto's feet.

The women gather in the living room every Thursday night with old grocery bags filled with cotton thread and needles. Threads of her father's story slip from the women's mouths in slow and deliberate loops, like the rosettes that appear between Mara's fingers from the cotton sifting around her crochet needle. They talk to her like she's a child hearing about Red Riding Hood.

"There were two brothers, Giorgio, who is your father, and Tommaso, who was the oldest, the barber. Tommaso was political, you know how barbers like to talk, discussing politics while he's steaming towels and leathering up faces with foam. He even had a press at the back of the shop. And Giorgio, *stupido*," the cousin shrugs, her voice bending her father's name with a musical lilt, "he wanted to do what his older brother did, so he went to the street and he passed out the fliers."

She pops forward, the needle clanging from her lap onto the floor. "But he didn't know how to recognize a Fascist from the others, and so…"

An aunt tells Mara, "Don't go telling your friends about this, now."

So what, Mara thinks. Everyone's father is a ghost, a soldier on the front, a letter, a patriot, a victim of Hitler or Mussolini, or else a Communist or a Socialist on the run: a red.

The aunts says, "It's not something you want to talk about, your father going to jail: *una ragazza per bene* doesn't want it known that her father was a red. You want a clean reputation."

And yet, in her aunt's voice she detects a sweet, faint lilt, like in a song, even as the warning is sharp, reminding her, "Tell no one of this. It's our business."

"And your mother," says the cousin, shrugging as if the ghost of a great-grandmother were sitting there whispering, don't say it, "she used to go to the jailhouse with a picnic basket, with the other women from the resistance, and they'd sit out in the grass and sing Bella Ciao or *Quel Mazzolin' di Fiori*." Her aunt puckers her lips as she sings the last part, batting eyelashes at the ceiling. "But they changed the words, you see. They worked them into codes so that they could tell each other who was arrested, who escaped, who was killed, you know, that way they could send each other messages."

Aunt Marta folds her lips, squints at the crochet needle, says, "That *disgraziata*. She was already pregnant with you." Her fingertips fold closed, her hand bobbing.

Mara feels the words clutching her chest, pulling on her tummy. She was there, too: a swelling under her mother's apron, a promise between them, and a worry, a kick from inside, perhaps, when the prison guards loaded their guns and shot at her feet, saying, "Go picnic somewhere else. This isn't a place for mothers."

Often, Giorgio wakes them all up at night gasping, choking on his own shouts about the rolling tanks. He says his fingers are burning, and he holds his hands up and stares at them, without seeing them, the fingers curled like claws on his face. Mara stands in the doorway, the light from behind her elongating her shadow.

"What is it now?"

"Go back to sleep, Mara."

"I can't sleep with him screaming like that."

Her mother, with her arms still coiled around the heavy-breathing soldier, strokes his head with a "Shhh. You're scaring la bambina, see?"

Mara tries to think of him as her father, her *babbo*, but he's Giorgio, the soldier, the stranger. He screams at night.

Her mother pushes aside her blankets. The sigh from her lips is almost enough to tell Mara too much about intimacy between men and women. Her long, naked feet slap on the cold tile.

"He's only dreaming," Mother coos, her hand light on her head. But the soldier's eyes are wide open, shiny with a fear chiseled and sharp like a diamond, glowing with dread in the pitch dark.

The door closes shut on him. Her mother's breath smells of chamomile; her robe is woolly and hopeful with perpetually blooming marigolds, but Mara carries the image of the soldier to bed with her, his shining eyes popping sprays of dirt.

His head, shaved to the skin of his scalp, seems bloodless, the bones protruding stubbornly and tapering off at his temples and high forehead, as though the whole of his bones cling to his soul, his famine-tortured, to his soul, fatless muscle tissue and tendons, keeping him anchored into his nightmares, the ghosts of his mysterious war pushing into life from under his taut, exhausted skin. The mouth, open and dry and black inside with German curses, follow both Mara and her mother to the sofa in the living room where Mara sleeps alone.

The war takes things from children: white bread and meat for dinner, for example, gifts at Christmas and birthdays, safety in a grandfather's embrace, and of course, fathers. When her mother clings to the sweating Giorgio, her hurried whispers exchanged against his panic-infused shouts, Mara knows her mother is taken, too.

Her father is an old, fading photograph propped on her mother's dresser in which he's slender like a stag in the black and white. He's a uniform, a regret, a sigh in the mouths of the old aunts, a whimper in her mother's nightmares, an optimistic ghost trapped in a frame, her soldier father, smiling always. In her living room, her aunt brings out the pictures, the only ones that are left, out of coincidence, untouched by the small disasters of a country in turmoil. The other aunts look up only momentarily from their needlework; then they look at each other with silent understanding.

Her aunt says, "He was a boxer, your father. Welter- Weight.

As a young man, before the war, he even won a belt." She passes the box of pictures to Mara, even as she clings to her crochet needle and looks down at the rectangular coaster she hopes to turn into a party favor.

She opens the unremarkable water-stained box, and lifts from it a studio picture, well preserved, though its corners curl at the edges.

"This one was in a book about Welter-Weight champions." Her aunt shrugs, her mouth tugging down with her pride.

He's eternally young, her father: so chiseled clean, his blue eyes peering with intensity behind the propped up boxing gloves, his pretense-ferociousness making him seem like a Hollywood star, destined to break women's hearts only with kisses.

"The Fascists were bastards, but not like the Nazi's," says her cousin. "So at sixteen, Giorgio was too young for torture. But Tommaso," the cousin waves her hand to the ceiling, her eyes rolling back, "eh!" she says with an odd certainty, "he was already in his twenties. The Fascists, they used everything, from boots with cleats pressing on testicles, to bottles of Ricin oil to make you shit your soul and pride– anything to crack a man from the carapace of his dignity."

"And babbo?" Mara pretends to be looping the needle to close the chain, but she wants only to know about the ghost that populates the dreams of her mother.

The women shake their head, and offer their scowls to their clicking needles: "That's why Giorgio joined the resistance," one says, and shrugs. "They put your father in the next room: for hours he had to sit on a wooden bench with his ear too close to the paper-thin walls, hearing Tommaso, *poverino*, crying, begging for his life."

Not yet eleven, Mara dreams of school dances and beauty contests, worries over the Latin test and the pen that her best friend lost down the face of the promontory, the steel-tipped stylus which Mara is foolish enough to recover for her. She ducks under the wired fence, ripping her skirt in the thorns. She slides down the steep slope in her good Mary-Janes, staining her socks and scraping her knees on the jutting rocks.

In class, the false accusations rise in whispers behind her back. The rip in her clothes, the dirty socks and shoes are evidence enough for her schoolmates.

Una ragazza per bene...needs a clean reputation.

"I was only trying to recover a stylus pen," she says to the glinting small teeth of the other girls.

At night, though, the table is set for three, and dinner is eaten tight mouthed, her mother hissing, "Eat! Before it gets cold," to Mara's: "Where is *Babbo*?"

When her mother first met her father, she belonged to the Daughters of Mary, happy to wear a uniform and parade for Mussolini's Italy, holding up flags and singing songs for the glory of the Mother of God. Then one day as she and the girls strolled down Via Nazionale, Giorgio stood there in his army uniform with other men not nearly as pretty as he, and after she passed, turning a nervous chuckle to her teasing friend, she noticed that he now strutted after her, pretending business with the same gelateria. He paid for her cone, and after she thanked him, he whistled just loud enough not to be too rude.

But in Piombino women have always spoken to each other from window to window, gossip bouncing from balcony to street as they hang their clothes or carry the groceries back home:

Nonna Marina saw the wife of her third cousin passing, leaned down to be heard:

Ciao Gina, did you find fresh apricots at the market? Last time I was there they were still too green.

I didn't go to the market this time. I went to Pino's in Piazza Bovio and saw your daughter. She was talking to the Cateni boy. You know he's on leave.

No sooner had Liliana stepped through the door than Nonna Marina pounced on her with a finger pushing against her breastbones.

"Don't you dare! That boy's sister's engagement was broken because the older brother went to jail. That whole family is red."

"What does it mean, red?"

But Nonno Egisto stood up, a hand clutching the top button of his brown cardigan sweater. He pulled on his good ear, and then on the other ear, the one that was ruined when he got sick with malaria, at fifteen, working to drain the Maremma for Mussolini.

"I know what it means, I do," he said, punching the front pocket of his shirt. He nodded, his eyes rolling up. "You chose well, Liliana, you did."

Most nights Giorgio's tenor voice fills the evening with song, his fingers banging on a table, or pushing the white and black keys of an accordion. Then it seems to Mara that the war has never happened, that Italy isn't still struggling to make sense of itself with cudgels and clenched fists, and that her mother and she have always danced together like this, their shiny black shoes scraping against the waxed floor, their skirts swirling around their knees, and Giorgio, *Babbo*, bending his head as he sings to them, the accordion breathing love.

Her *babbo*, at the door, is shredded like an old cloth. Cuts over his eyebrows are darkened with healing, the skin already swelling, wet around the gashes. He is crowded by a small mob of his comrades who call out, *Dai, Giorgio, dai*. His arms are badly bandaged with old rags, the torn pieces of his shirt.

Wool-capped men rumble vociferously, streaming in behind him.

"Liliana, get your husband wine. He almost died saving the mill today. Get in, *dai Giorgio*." They wave as if directing traffic, ignoring her mother's "*Madonnina, c'hai fatto?*"

At eleven, with her breasts already formed, Mara knows that men exaggerate, but *Babbo's* wounds stain his coat, and the ironed and bleached shirt and undershirt. His boasts are filled with more than just the puerile hopes of hormonal boys, and Mara is touched by the cold prospect of an inconsiderate fear: the dank stink of death breathing down her father's spine.

"The plant almost exploded," he says. "It was a narrow escape." He talks loud, his voice cracking with his laughter. He explains he'd fallen asleep. It was his job to watch the temperature gauge, and to turn off the furnace when the heat got too high. He'd been working late shifts, taking on his comrade's hours so that he could attend the party meeting the next day.

"The party meeting..." Liliana's chin tilts in an unspoken accusation.

It was lucky he fell off his chair, he says. He woke up just in time. Or almost just in time. "There was no time for me to run through the hallway and down to the control room. I had to take a short cut through the glass, ha, ha."

He laughs big, his head thrown back, his mouth open and showing his teeth. The men who share his wine in thick water glasses, nod, confirming the story adding their own details: the high pitched whistle from the boilers, the tipped cauldron, the flow of melted ore, the crash of breaking glass. They talk at once, their voices clapping with consonants, the vowels stretching large with their respect. Glass shards in her father's hair gleam as the light strikes them, sharp like his eyes.

"And you," he says, his eyebrows meeting at the bridge of his straight nose.

"I heard you broke a boy's skull with a perfume bottle."

"He tried to kiss me!"

"You see? My daughter is a fighter."

The men bray like donkeys. Her father goes to the pantry, and from the wooden crate he takes a green bottle of wine, already empty. He holds it up like a trophy.

"And next time, use this!"

But the next thing she remembers is looking out the window up at that huge round moon, glowing red behind a curtain of silver grey clouds.

Luna rossa, o piscia o soffia, the Tuscan proverb rings in her head, a bad omen, a shiver of storms, and just then the doorbell buzzes, inside her head and out in the cool night.

She looks down. The sidewalk is dotted with iron gray hair, buns, tails, foulards tied under chins and a woman calls out, "Mara, apri!" Open up; it's only us.

The women who come wear long coats. Scarves. Gloves. So black and threadbare that when they breeze past her through the door, the cold emanates from their corpulence. The women go straight to the kitchen. One takes a kettle out and fills it with water to boil. Another wraps an arm around Mara and says, "Be a good girl. Go downstairs for a minute, and wait for your mother."

Liliana in her night robe demands, "Oh, *Madonnina*, tell me the truth. Tell me the truth, damn it. Something happened."

The women sit her down, hands in her hair, on her shoulder, stroking her elbows as they warn, "*Calmati*, Liliana, *calmati*." Their mouths smell of badly chewed lies.

Mara moves out of their sweeping bodies, steps downstairs and into the lobby, and slips through the open portal so quietly that the women standing at the corner, one smoking, the other looking across the street as if on a lookout for someone, keep talking, never noticing her. Liliana's cries reek from the window above.

"Why is she screaming like that," asks the smoking woman to the other. "Is Giorgio hurt that badly?" Her chin tilts up, and Mara sees her blanched skin: in the moonlight, the folds under her dark eyes are stained an oily yellow. The women's shadows conflate on the sidewalk, on the street.

Mara's breath condenses before her lips, leaving evidence of her numbness before it disperses.

She thinks she can see it as it happened, the darkened road in the hills, the soft buzzing of the scooter on the way home from a party meeting. The driver thinks he sees a light shining from the hills. An outpost of the Fascist! The party cards in their shirt pockets, the red bands tied around their necks!

The moped jolts suddenly. The front wheel spins, and Giorgio is bucked: like a sack from a tired mule pitching a fit. There are still so many black shirts, patrolling roads at night, waiting like wolves for the chance to return. The driver dislocates his knee, his ankle is twisted, too. It's dark, and he thinks he sees shadows flitting from trees, the bushes, soughing threats.

"Giorgio!" he shout-whispers. He can't be sure what he hears, the muted voices of conspiracy, perhaps; the clicking of hunting rifles. "Giorgio! Giorgio!"

Mara dreams of two lovers, kissing in the bed car on a train, headed for a beach hotel in Sorrento. The train hisses to a halt. The tin-voice of the officials resounds in the sudden quiet, the hush of the engine aberrant. A man in a brown shirt and uniform moves from car to car, asking for papers.

"Documents, please, documents."

The lovers hear his voice, the train cars opening and slamming on their rails. An old woman complains, "Can't you see my son is too young to be in the military? He's hardly twelve."

Giorgio sighs and rolls his eyes. He reaches up for his papers in the pocket of his jacket.

"*Congedato*," he says to the man in uniform who eyes the tough muscles on his arms scarred with the memories of war. "On leave," Giorgio repeats. "I just got married a few hours ago."

By the time they reach the beach, it is already late, the contours of the hills brilliant against the setting sun. But the sea clacks stones together as it rakes the shore, its foaming whispers inviting the newlyweds to forget.

Giorgio's hair is plastered to his forehead, his wide blue eyes like glass, like wet aquamarine, his teeth shining as he smiles. The water is tinseled gold with sunshine. Liliana's hands break the crest of oncoming waves. Spray rises around her, a rainbow of laughter and droplets haloing them. The setting sun threads bruises through the clouds. Liliana touches her hand and knows with a crack in her chest that her wedding band, slightly oversized, is gone, slipped from her finger as she was playing, lost to the immense, darkening sea.

"Oh God." A hand clings to her finger; her finger touches her lips.

Mara imagines it like this: Giorgio diving and diving again under the water, everything below shining with the promise of re-demption, smooth, polished black stones, pieces of glass rendered dull by the patience of waves, the shiny skin of smelts – everything. Liliana, shivering alone, wet on the shore, watches him disappear below the surface of the sea, not knowing this is how it will be from now on, catching glimpses of him as his glimmering back breaks the surface and his head emerges, throwing back a tuft of drenched hair, he explodes a breath for his lungs, and then again, he dips be-low the surface, one with the swelling sea, the clouds, the inevitable chill of night.

Lumache con Polenta-Snails on Grit Cakes

Grits are coarsely ground dried corn. So is polenta, though it is ground a little more finely. Do not use cornmeal or instant grits for this recipe, as they have little substance or mouth feel to them.

For Polenta:

4 cups milk
1 cup real stone ground yellow grits or yellow polenta
Salt and pepper
½ cup fresh grated grana Padano cheese
2 tbsp lard or bacon fat for frying

The night before serving the meal: Bring milk to simmer, avoiding a scald. Add grits or polenta, return milk to a simmer and reduce heat to low. Stir frequently to keep grits from sticking or burning, for about 45 minutes or until soft to the bite. You may need to add more milk. If so, add it by the tablespoon. Stir in cheese. Remove from heat and pour into a well-oiled 9x13 glass-baking dish. Cover and refrigerate overnight.

Cut the grits/polenta into triangular cakes. Bring fat to 350 degrees and fry cakes till browned on both sides. Place on a plate and spoon the snail mixture over them. Serve immediately. If you have polenta cakes left over, wrap them in kitchen film, bag them and freeze them.

For Snails:

1 can large wild burgundy snails, drained and rinsed several times
2 tbsp dry white wine
½ stick butter, cut into small cubes
2 tbsp cream
3 slices of pancetta, cut into thin, short ribbons and gently fried (not crispy)
1 tbsp anchovy paste
2 shallots, finely chopped
2 fresh sage leaves, finely chopped
I/2 roma tomato, finely chopped
2 tbsp chopped chives
salt and pepper to taste

Place wine, shallots, sage leaves, and anchovy paste in a cold sauté pan. Turn on heat, bring to a simmer and let simmer till shallots are soft, 5-6 minutes. Add cream.

Lower heat and whisk in cold butter, one small cube at a time. Once incorporated, add the snails and bacon, salt and pepper. Heat gently until snails are warmed through. Add tomatoes and chives, and transfer immediately to serving bowl.

Remedy for finding a lost object:

To find a lost object, one must turn an open heart to St. Anthony and recite the Hail Mary thirteen times, repeating each line of the prayer twice. If the lost object is a wedding ring, to avoid bad luck in the marriage, the spouse of the person who lost the wedding ring must buy a new wedding band right away, and place it on the finger of the loved one as one did during the wedding ceremony.

Suffer The Children

The devil lives in Sardinia. That's what the legends say. The devil got tired of Hell, so when he heard this restless sea, crushing and foaming against the jagged rockface, and when he saw the thorny creepers and poisoned plants clinging in patches to the dusty hills, he crawled out of hell and emerged into the blinding sun from the nurage cave-dwellings abandoned six millennias ago and took up shop. If you ask the women, they say they've seen tracks of fire where the devil's hooves pass. If you ask the herders, they complain that the devil stole their cattle and then turned the beasts into red ants just for mischief. And if you ask the old men, they chew on the ends of their pipes and say nothing for a while, although one might massage a handful of sweaty cards and nod, slowly, as if swaying to an old song, and maybe, if his wine glass is half full he might say he's seen what he thinks was the devil's winged shadow pass over him once. And everyone will tell you: the devil's minions scuttle from house to house to scratch prophecies of doom on the window shutters of an unlucky home.

"Because," an old woman says, "when a murderer gets away from the law, the devil catches up to him, and turns him into a demon in the shape of a goat, and then that demon will be restless all night, scratching its horns on the window shutters where a baby might die in his sleep, or where a young girl will lose her virginity before she's married."

Ask the foreigners from the mainland, the families like ours, who come only in summer from Milan, Bologna, or Rome, and they will say, "What devil? Not even the Pope believes in the devil anymore."

Ask the children, and they will tell you Sardinia is paradise, and if there's a devil, for certain, he must be that school teacher, Mr. Duri, who always yells at the kids and scares them off his property clutching a rake.

Our Sardinia was, anyway, the final destination of a trip we looked forward to all year, since the first day of school in the first week of September, and then again from after Easter to June, and with particularly frenzied spirits through that long stretch of time when there was nothing more to look forward to but summer. And the long trip of two days and the cleaning of the tightly shuttered "villino" that smelled like dust and was already infested with country mice was nothing more than an inconvenience to our residence near a vast and quiet beach, with diaphanous blue waters, and sparsely visited expanses of dune grass and sand.

We were six, nine and twelve when my parents first bought that tight little cottage improperly called "little villa" on the Sardinian cove of Costa Rei. The front yard was all cacti and ice plant, and the beach rose in crystalline white dunes and sloped into the mouth of a transparent blue sea just a few yards from our front porch. The only devil was the threat of moray eels in the cluster or rocks that jutted out here and there in shallows. We were told not to swim by the rocks, that the snorkeling gear and the movement of our feet might get one of those underwater serpents angry. But of course, we swam there anyway.

There were only a dozen other cottages in Costa Rei, each one looking exactly like ours: three bedrooms, a living room with glass doors, a sun porch and a fireplace. There was nothing around but a dirt road. Unless someone wanted to count the pizza joint seven miles north, the nearest sources of groceries were the cattle farms on the nearby hills. We could have suckling pig, duckling, and baby goat slaughtered for a modest price; we could drink raw milk, and eat jelly we'd boiled from the raspberries that grew on the wild bushes all around. That was the price to pay for only one channel of tv and a scarce selection of toys snuck in the trunk of the Renault 16, which every summer shuttled us from our home in Milan to the port of Civitavecchia, and onto the groaning ship that ferried us into the Cagliari port.

There were kids from other families whom we saw summer after summer. We were a hydra of a twenty-faced brat pack with three or four leaders acting as an alternate head. We were middle-class urchins from cities of industry and crowd, eager to shed urban propriety along with our clothes. We dared each other to tiptoe barefooted over a thirty feet stretch of pebble path; we ran through dune grass and fields of bamboo until, breathless, we leaped fast over the scorching sand, diving into the blue with the displaced water greeting us with its cool currents. With brine in our hair and sand under our fingernails, we collected starfish and shells and spiraled stones we called St Lucy's Eye, and we dove underwater to fish cracked terracotta jars abandoned by who knows what past century's galleon.

Perhaps the devil came to this paradise because he wanted privacy: the sun burned our skin at noon, and at night, without movie theaters, restaurants, or even a fairly stocked supermarket we only had ourselves for entertainment. Who knows, it might have been a good place for the devil to be, with so much boredom egging us on.

We gathered with our parents on our tiled sun porches for card-tournaments with kilos of ash-roasted baby pig and baked potatoes, to celebrate island scarcity with wine, fresh seafood and songs by Mina and Gianni Morandi. Summer time was for the living. Time to shake the hips, and clap, and call it dancing, and when the adults weren't looking, *Check out Fabrizio's butt in those jeans, and look, Pietro lost weight again. Bet he'll gain it back in a couple of hours tonight*, until, *I think I ate too much* rubbing the back of a hand over the belly, *Mamma, I'm tired.*

Shut up. It's hardly seven. You go to sleep now you'll be up be-

fore dawn.

But I'm sleepy.

Go rest on the couch and leave me alone.

And we kids yawned and watched our parents call out to each other the invented virtues of their sons and daughters, along with pinochle trumps and the tallying of scores. Then it was time to cluster noiselessly out on the porch, curing boredom with ghost stories, *Well, everyone's done the Ouija, with the little glass, but that's kid's stuff,* the kind forbidden by Catholic nuns, *I'm talking about possessions here,* as if our lives were not uncertain enough, *You've got to be big like me, at least in the tenth grade,* that we needed ghosts to validate us, *It's not for little kids with milk on the lips like you, tiny buns,* to test our prepubescent courage, *You'd start crying and you'd chase away the ghost.* Or worse, to swap a yawn for a shiver: *You'd bring the devil. Yeah, I said the devil. You think it's funny, do you?*

That's when we turned to Lucia, the long-haired girl with the freckles and the pretty far-away eyes, the girl who looked at you without looking at you, whose voice was always a breath or two after her words. Lucia already spoke like she belonged to the ghosts, her long hair sweeping over the table, her hands shifting this way and that. She told us how the spirits visited her at night, how they woke her up with nightmares. She told us about the drowned girl whose spirit slipped inside her nostrils, tying up her tongue and flouncing her about like a Neapolitan puppet. *Dangerous,* she tantalized us. *You can't imagine how.*

But the next morning, when the talk was sharpened by the heat and the salt, the older kids said other things. They said Lucia was one of the "absent ones," that she was headed for "a bad finale." Lucia, who dressed in men's suits three times her size, this girl who was caught at night drinking and sucking up joints: everyone knew that her mother couldn't stop her, and her father, the Alitalia pilot, was too busy womanizing to bother. Who was there to stop Lucia, who ran away at night sneaking through the window, such a pretty red-haired girl with wide green eyes, headed for a bad finale? We envied Lucia's long eyelashes and the happy red strands of her hair, but we certainly didn't envy those rumors that followed her, rising after each of her footsteps like a black puff of dust.

"Ghosts?" The boys laughed. "She sleeps all day because she's poking herself."

The boys pushed on their veins and wiggled an eyebrow. And you were supposed to understand, even if you were a little one, that Lucia was a heroin addict, she and her ghost stories and her tragic family: her mother who drank, her father who cheated, her brother Fabrizio who was a delinquent and failed all his classes (at fifteen, he was still in the eight grade), and little Marzio, the youngest, who had turned stupid from taking so many hits on the head from his drunk mother.

Lucia's family lived in a little stucco cottage identical to all of ours, complete with solarium and draping bougainvillea, it's coarse, shepherd-style, chestnut-wood furniture a duplicate reflection of ours. When Lucia had a date, we watched her preening her long red hair looking at herself through the reflection on the glass door. We'd shake our head at Lucia the beautiful for wearing those foolish-looking pant suits, and she threw us a smile through the window reflection, and sometimes even asked us, "How do I look?" not realizing we were too shy to tell her that girls weren't supposed to wear boys' clothes, that jackets and ties on a girl didn't look so good, and she was *pazza!*, crazy-crazy for asking us. But we nodded, because our mothers had taught us that in somebody else's house you had to be polite, and we said that she looked beautiful. She glanced at herself then, smoothing her lips with a wet finger, mussing a curl around her sweet oval face.

"Lucia, tell us about ghosts? Play the *medium* for us, for a spiritual sitting."

Lucia cursed, her hands slapping her thighs: "I shouldn't have said anything. You think it's a joke? You have to take things with respect, otherwise you can call on the devil. Once the devil is in your house, *belle mie*, you can never get rid of him."

"We'll be careful, we promise."

"Oh, you promise, do you?"

"Please, Lucia. We want to talk to ghosts."

"What do you think the ghosts can tell you? They're dead."

But we didn't care what they told us: only that we could ask them questions and see for ourselves all the things the Catholic nuns had warned us against.

"You, Lucia, you can ask the ghosts good questions. Everyone knows you are the best psychic here."

"No, no," she waved her long finger at us, puckering her mouth in the process. "When kids call on ghosts they get stupid and laugh. If you laugh, you attract negative spirits, maybe even the devil. And who will pay for it, huh? I will! Because I will be in a trance. This is serious stuff. Forget it, *bambine*."

But sometimes if she didn't have a red Fiat or a metal-blue Alfa parked near her window, waiting to take her we-could-not-imagine-where, then she'd come and sit with us on the front porch under the flowering bougainvillea to drink fizzy sugar water, and listen to us talk about who kissed the softest after the bottle spun, who still sported the stinging slap of a mother's sandal, and who had split that palm frond without being shot with salt in the butt by Mr. Duri.

We sat around in the evening, sighing for adventure, impatient for morning, spitting *gazzosa* at each other and sporting our tanned bellies with short cut shirts and low slacks when someone brought up the ghosts.

Lucia spoke in a quiet voice: "Once at a chain sitting, someone broke the chain. I was sitting right next to her. Up to then, we'd felt Spirit spinning like a centrifuge from body to body as we held hands. But the girl next to me, I don't know, maybe she was scared, maybe she just didn't know any better. She let go. I felt Spirit gathering up in my chest, so strong it threw me back. I buckled and heaved, trying to throw up. I cannot describe it to you, how I jerked and flailed, and they had to hold me down until morning. I cried so hard after that. So hard."

We were sitting on the edge of the chairs, playing with straws and bottle labels. "Tell us more," we wanted to say, but the questions were taken from our mouths and shoved in the messy drawer of our imaginations.

"Anyway, we shouldn't be talking about this," said Lucia. "It's bad luck to talk about Spirit like this."

"Bullshit," said Pietro. "It was just you doing all that to yourself. Maybe you were drunk again, huh? But probably, you were high."

Maybe it was magic, or maybe it was, as we all told each other later, just a coincidence, but Lucia was still saying, "Don't say that, Pietro. It makes Spirit mad," when the lights flickered a little on our front porch and after a collective ahhh, we were plunged into darkness.

We hushed, but the cicadas screamed a little louder.

Pietro said, "Ooooh. Here comes Spirit. Watch out."

"Shut up, stupid. Don't make fun of Spirit like that."

"Spirit is bullshit," said Pietro.

Somebody said, "Stop it, Pietro."

Pietro cackled and said, "Spirit is a juvenile dickhead, playing with the light switch."

The light bulb flickered on. Lucia had leaned back on her elbows, her wide green eyes shifting from Pietro to the light bulb.

Pietro had a reputation for being good at making people "dick-off like a bull," pushing on someone's buttons until those buttons popped off and hit you in the teeth. The mothers said it was because he was overweight and had an insecurity complex. (They said that only when Pietro's mother wasn't around). They said he did it just to show that he was somebody. And he always got the other kids, the good children, the innocent lambs -- he always got them "in an ugly situation." But try to remind a mother of that when her sandal is in mid flight sailing towards your head. She'd say, "Me? I would never say that about a child!" And for that, you'd get the other sandal, too.

"So what that the light went out," Pietro said, his voice like an out of tune mandolin. "It happens."

Maybe it was the workers at the power plant who weren't getting it right, or maybe Spirit didn't like Pietro any more then Lucia liked him. We didn't know. But certainly, we knew we had no power.

"Spirit, we apologize for Pietro," we heard Lucia mutter. "He doesn't know better. Spirit, we ask that you restore the power in this house."

The generators hummed on the last vowel of Lucia's words, and the lights flickered on.

We clapped and looked at Lucia, who hung back with a satisfied expression reserved for Pietro. But Pietro produced a smug smile, his fatty cheeks pushing over his cheekbones, making his giblet eyes look even smaller.

"Yeah, Spirit, suck my cock!"

We saw Lucia reach over the table for Pietro, we heard the smack of her hand on his naked arm, and heard him shout, "Ouch!" but we couldn't see. The hum of generators quieted suddenly and the light cut off, adding spike to our punch-cocktail of boredom and imagination.

"Pietro," we screamed.

"This is a fucking island. It's just a blackout."

Lucia pushed away from the table, all choked up and ruffled.

"I pay for this," she said, pointing at Pietro. "That's why I don't like to talk about this stuff with kids. Then Spirit takes it out on me."

Had we been any older we might have realized that the way her lips tensed wasn't so much a frown as it was an attempt to hold back the pleasure she felt for the respect she had garnered in that one session of light flickering. But now that we had witnessed the Almighty Light Withdrawal, there was no mission nobler than persuading Lucia to lead off a "seduta spiritica."

For weeks, the only thing that came out of our mouths was the night that the lights went out because Pietro made fun of Spirit. All we needed was little Marzio's official report that he saw Lucia the next morning on the floor of her bedroom, naked and beaded in sweat, her eyes rolling back in her head, her mouth coated in saliva, a gasping not unlike that of lovemaking heaving through her chest and throat. It convinced us without a breath of doubt that Lucia had been punished by Spirit on Pietro's account, even if the adults dismissed this tale as yet more evidence that the Della Rosa girl was a junkie, a "*drogata*" headed for "a bad finale."

Then Giovanna arrived from Cagliari and that's when things got interesting.

She was a Sardinian, with an olive complexion that turned dark after only just an hour of sun, and she lived in Cagliari, the only big city on the island, a short afternoon drive away. We'd known her since our village in Costa Rei was just a spatter of rocks and shrubs near the beach. There were only twelve cottages back when we'd first moved in, and she had already lived there long before the Duris arrived with their dour dislike of kids, or the Della Rosas with their drama of dysfunctionality and womanizing. She was there before us, before any of the ones who became regular, at first only a lonely girl with a large straw hat and hair that reached all the way to the well of her back.

She had no shyness at all, nor any manners that any Italian mother could approve of. She strolled one day on the ice plant on our front yard and up the garden terrace wearing a bikini bottom, flip flops, and a toothy smile. She went straight for the only near-age girl she saw, Vittoria, who was reading *The Black Corsair* while leaning against the stucco pillar solarium and took a long time to realize that there even was someone talking to her at all.

"Giovanna," she said by way of introduction, foregoing the hello, foregoing the clarification that she was, in fact, talking about herself. A mastiff pup trotted behind her, slobbering and shifting his round eyes from Vittoria to her, while at the same time, wagging its short tail.

"Is that your dog?" Vittoria asked.

Giovanna looked over her shoulder like she'd forgotten the pup. "It belongs to that German lady who lives in the villa behind you. She's teaching me German in exchange for my walking her dog."

"Can I walk it with you?"

Mamma came out on the porch with her hair gathered in a kerchief tied up on the top in a flourishing ribbon. She held a mop and a bucket. She wore a tshirt and shorts and flip flops. She looked at Giovanna's hat, then at her naked breasts. Giovanna was fourteen, maybe. Mamma's smile scrambled and flipped over like a frittata.

Giovanna said, "Do you have anything to drink, Signora? It's hot out here."

It was settled. Giovanna was a slut, and Vittoria shouldn't be friends with her. But this was Sardinia, of course, and summertime. On an island, either one runs with the pack or one is run out of town by it. Mamma might say, "There's something ugly about that Giovanna, and certainly I don't like the way she goes around showing her tits to everyone." But she was powerless against the draw of the pack.

Besides, when Mamma became friends with Pietro's mother and was therefore initiated in her own pack, sunbathing without a top became fashionable, and if those sphere-eyed goat herders drove their sheep from the hills to the beach just so they could stare at tits, then it was unconscionable that there could still be Italians in this day and age that would get excited over women's breasts. How ignorant. How a sign of poverty and backwardness!

When we were all still little, so little that our mothers still fed us Nutella on bread for snacks, we used to sigh after Giovanna's long auburn hair and her skinny legs, and we didn't see the low forehead, the mean small eyes, the pimples and the weak chin. This went on for years, until Pietro called it out that not only was Giovanna ugly, but also a bitch, especially since she had taken to smoking.

Even so, those afternoons that we walked the four miles uphill to the new beach hotel for the disco dance for minors, the boys lined up to dance with her all the same. Pietro said that the bouquet of whitehead blooming periodically on the well of her chin were "clear evidence" that she wasn't a virgin, but that didn't stop him from walking her mastiffs and stealing her shirt on the beach so she would chase after him fast into the water, and then he'd have an excuse to wrap his arms around her and hold her a while.

Giovanna was like a shaken fizzy water bottle, like when we held the thumb on the tip and pointed it at the boys if they acted stupid. She was the sticky spray, the icy cold surprise, the gooey sugar stain on our brown calves. When Giovanna arrived, things happened. If we played spin the bottle, she insisted on more than kisses: one night Fabrizio pulled down his jeans and showed us his penis by moonlight after the bottle settled on his flip flop, and though bored he was, and though the flashlight showed only bits of his penis at a time, he obliged and declared with a grin: "This is too much for you little girls."

"Giovanna! Where have you been! Pietro dared Spirit and the lights went out!"

"I went to Germany," Giovanna said, rolling her eyes. Already her attention was elsewhere, her nose veering suddenly to the left as she snorted.

We talked really fast, and all at once, explaining Pietro, explaining Lucia, the power outage and the flickering lights with our fingers flying and our spit arcing towards her chin. She snorted, called out to the pack of mastiff rolling and playing at her feet orders in German: "Platz! Platz!"

"Get to the point," she said, waving her hand.

"Tell her, Marzio, tell her about what you saw the next day."

But Marzio stuttered when he got nervous. "I saw ...I... sssss-saw... bbut...bbbbbbut...and then..." He sighed as if he'd just climbed up to the top of the hill without a straw hat, and he stuffed his thumb in his mouth while with his other hand he rubbed the top of his head in soothing circles.

"Anybody can be a *medium*," Giovanna yawned. "Hell, I could be a medium if I wanted to, especially if you paid me."

"Nohhh," we waved our hands before her face, competing with each other to clarify the situation, except for Marzio who had removed the thumb from his mouth and pointed it at her, the thing glistening with sunshine and saliva: "Nnnno. Mmmmmy ssssister..."

Giovanna clicked her tongue. She turned back to her mastiffs, riling them up to tail-wagging attention with a snap of her fingers, then without even bothering to look over her shoulder she said, "Get me when you all grow up."

At night, while the adults proceeded oblivious with their dinner card nights and Marilyn Monroe movie nights, we avoided talking about ghosts. Instead we talked about Giovanna's demonstrations of her mastiff's identity crisis, and how she hunkered down on all fours for him, laughing when the confused dog tried to mount her.

It made us feel better to point out her slutty shamefacedness for the fact that she often shunned us to hang out instead with those hated German tourists, whom we blamed for having mistaken Sardinia for their personal nudist beach and for the frequent forest fires that happened during the dry summers. We had all noticed how, whenever one of those fires seared up another slice of hill, some bleached German investor would end up buying the burnt up land and build another villa.

Now our private paradise crowded the hills and the shore with several thousands of identical-looking villas, and for this we blamed these harsh-speaking, sausage-loving people -- whom we had a duty to despise on account of what they did to Italy during World War II. But for Giovanna to prefer the company of Germans to us, for her to favor their sun-exposed genitalia was insult greater than we could bear, and we drank up bitterness with our sugared fizzy water, remembering her insults and enlarging them with our gossip.

Something of Giovanna's skepticism must have spread on our consciousness like a rash. Too demoralized to bring up the ghosts with Lucia again, we focused our efforts instead on stuffing plastic sandwich bags filled with sand and water into the gas tanks of those ill-fated weekend-dwellers whom we considered intruders. They came to our beach and left gelato wrappers floating like jellyfish on our diaphanous sea, and we appointed ourselves judges and executioners. Otherwise, we'd give ourselves projects: ripping up Mr. Duri's bougainvillea when the man was away; building rubber band guns with bamboo canes and clothes pins; teasing to tears a rather large group of Sardinian locals whose families had piled up together in one cottage, possibly come on this side of the island to be gardeners and house-keepers to the richer cottage owners.

On the outside we were a cheerful group of deeply tanned savages in fabric hats and Speedos, allowed to roam free with our parents' blessings. But on the inside we were dangerously bored, gritting our sand-speckled teeth at Giovanna's indifference and huffing around impatiently under Lucia's window.

At night, while the adults gathered in mosquito-safe kitchens, the clinking of the ice against their glasses fading proportionally to the rising volume of their laughter, we took to terrorizing the darkened home of the Sardinian pack. Of course it was entirely their fault. They ambushed us at the entrance of our bamboo coves and pelleted us with wet scarab balls (which became extraordinarily heavy when dipped in sea-water and made an odd, splattering sound when colliding with our heads). We vowed revenge and obtained it at night, posting vitriolic poems of Pietro's creation that made rhymes with the most unsightly body parts of the Sardinians girls, and by smearing their windows, doors, and car windshield with tree sap and Fabrizio's own lovingly donated cum.

Then we rang the doorbell.

And ran.

This went on for some nights, until the weaklings complained to our mothers. The Mothers came to the consensus that we had all gotten too cocky, and to rectify this alarming development, there was a vigorous raising and falling of the hands on our Speedoed

butts with harshly uttered pronouncements on our state of delin-
quency, until we apologized tear-faced to our shit-grin witnessing
enemies.

So that is how we found ourselves one night without projects,
enemies, or entertainment, lounging around in our living room,
and handling a deck of cards between us without any desire to play.
Giovanna strolled in from a walk on the beach with her mastiffs,
attracted by the light and the music playing. We watched her mastiffs romping and slobbering while DeAndre sang a Sardinian ballad in a Milanese accent so strong that nothing could have stood
as better evidence of the elitist northern academic background that
he boasted before his singing voice made him famous.

But Giovanna paid no attention to her mastiff nor to DeAndre's botching of her native dialect. Rather she kept grinning at
Lucia: "Ah, so, the medium is here. Have you called up any ghosts
yet?"

A quick glance, a nudging hand, and then all at once we chant-
ed, "Oh, please Lucia, please. You promised."

"We'll be good, we swear. We won't call up any bad ghosts."

"We want to see Spirit."

"We've been waiting all summer! Would you rather we did it
ourselves? Alone?"

"All right," Lucia relented. "Maybe it's better that I show you."

We rounded up cardboard and a small ashtray before Lucia
could change her mind, and we warned Giovanna that if she was
going to be *that way* she might as well walk in the rain back to
her villa, or to her German friends and see what *they* knew about
spirits. We drew letters and numbers in an oval spanning the full
length of a piece of cardboard. In the middle we drew two circles
with yes and no. Finally, we sat around the big dining room table
with our finger lightly resting on the thin glass ashtray that had to
serve as our planchette, while Lucia invoked Spirit.

"Spirit, if you are out there, please send us a sign.

'Spirit, if you are out there, please let us speak to you.

'Spirit, please reveal yourself; if you are here, let us know."

The clock ticked. One mastiff licked his balls. Another one farted.

We held our breaths, and we tried hard to keep our fingers light on the edges of the ashtray, careful not to cheat. Only Giovanna grinned, now and again producing a cough that sounded terribly much like a laugh. Lucia threw her hands up, her long strands of hair flying behind her.

"When skeptics are in the room, only devils come." She kicked her chair back, its legs scraping a howling sound against the tile.

One of the dogs got onto his feet and whined, pushing his flat face onto Giovanna's lap. She pushed him back and grabbed Lucia's wrist: "Come on, now," she said. "I'll behave."

Lucia looked at Giovanna a long time. What was she thinking? Was she thinking that Giovanna had gathered more popularity than she? Had she understood the laughter as a challenge? She allowed a minute to let our giggles wear out, and then recomposed herself, directing our fingers to the edges of the ashtray. She uttered a brief apology to Spirit and settled back into a trance-like quiet, her eyes closed, but rolling rapidly under her eyelids. She again intoned as before: "Spirit, if you are here, send us a sign."

She paused for a long while, her silence broken only by a short little gasp, and she whispered, "It's happening; I can feel him inside me."

The ashtray moved.

Only a little, but sharp like a shove.

"Welcome, Spirit. Talk to us?" Lucia's words broke up with her questions like the colors in the turning of a kaleidoscope wheel. We understood what she said not because of each particular word, but because of our collective mood.

The ashtray edged slightly towards the "yes."

"I can feel it," whispered Lucia. "This one is strong. Can we ask you questions?"

This time, the ashtray slid firmly to the "yes."

A choir of questions exploded from our collective mouths; we all wanted to know what was it like to be a spirit, what kind of spirit it was, where did it come from, what was it like in the other world, was it very, very painful to die? Was there really a God, and had the spirit seen Him? Could the spirit tell us the future?

The ashtray began to swing, at first gently, from the yes to the no and back again.

"Too many questions," said Lucia. "One at a time. Let's start by asking its name. Spirit, what is your name?"

The ashtray continued a slightly elliptic pattern between the *yes* and the *no*, picking up speed as we argued. It spun fast enough that some of us lost hold of it, at which point the ashtray would come to a hesitant pause enough for an accusation to fly: "Come on! Marzio has been pushing! I can feel him pushing from here!"

"Don't push. It confuses the spirit," said Lucia.

"I..I...I...I wasn't pu...pu....pu...pushing! My f..f...finger wasn't even t...t...t...t..touch...touching," managed Marzio. "L...l...look here! Look! I have my finger ab..b...b...bove the ashtray."

"Don't take your finger off!" Lucia gasped.

Too late. Marzio's thumb shoved deep inside his mouth, and his other hand grasped the hair on the nape of his neck.

Giovanna laughed. It was evil, the way the chortles throttled her breathing, the way her spit popped against air in the back of her throat. For a second or so, Giovanna's chortle was the only sound.

As if suddenly weakened by that laughter, the ashtray edged slowly, painfully, towards the letter S. Then it climbed back up and around the yes/no circles to turn left towards the letter A. Giovanna snorted just as the ashtray turned downward and edged again, with somewhat greater decisiveness on the T, angling upwards to the beginning of the alphabet, aiming for the A. Lucia shot up, her eyelids pushing back from her popping green eyes, her hands raised up to the sky: "Oh Lord and Little Madonna of Mine! Forgive us! Forgive us!"

We looked from face to face, wondering if it was all right now, to take our finger off the ashtray. The older kids had pushed their chairs back, their hands in their laps, their faces turned eagerly to

Lucia.

"It was trying to spell SATAN," someone whispered.

The ohhh's of our freshly enlightened acumens died in our lungs, extinguished immediately by the chilled hush of fear. After all, we'd all grown up with Baptism, Communion and Catechism, and we'd heard the S word hurled often enough at us from the pulpit to lose our milk teeth from chronic chattering.

Lucia cleared our hands off the table with a brief flutter of hers, and grabbing on to the hand-scribbled Ouija she ripped it in several pieces, reciting quick prayers and blowing on the broken edges each time before folding the pieces and ripping them anew. She invoked the Lord and Mary and Jesus and begged for their forgiveness, promising never to dabble again. When she was done, and the Ouija pieces burned in a plate on the table, and when the ashtray was ordered covered in salt and then discarded, she drew a long sigh, her eyes closed and her chin over her chest, her hair draping around her like the painting of a Raphaelite Madonna.

After moments stilled in this memorable pose, Lucia got up, and briskly dismissed herself. We didn't know it, then, but it was the last time we would ever see her.

A week after our sitting, we will hear news of the car accident from the whispers of the Twelve Mothers, Lucia driving home towards Rome in her boyfriend's Fiat 500, speeding fast towards her bad finale, drunk and with a split lip; it will take almost an entire day before anyone finds her car;

In the cupboard of the villa, dishes and glasses and plates will come flying from the kitchen cabinet where the fated and duly salted ashtray was replaced the very morning after the accident; we will vigorously proclaim it a coincidence to each other, saving our real thoughts for story-telling of years to come;

We will think our games against the Sardinians only games; we will think our illnesses and losses part of the normal hardships of life, and still we'll wonder;

Three baby magpies will be found dead in the backyard, each

impaled on the sharp, needled limbs of a century plant; we will fe-
rociously blame the Sardinian pack we had previously tormented,
and their morbid sense of vengeance.

And we will blame the Sardinians also for the strange noises that
we hear at night, noises like a goat rubbing its horns against the wood-
en hurricane shutters of our windows, noises accompanied by strange,
almost inhuman whispers, and the scraping of goat hooves on the roof.
We will say it was some disgruntled gardener who wanted work and
found none, some unhappy shepherd embittered by the ostentatious
sloth of the vacationers. We will even try to blame it on Pietro, who
will eventually land in juvie, who will stop speaking to us, by and by.

But at the villa the night took over with its crickets and cicadas, with its tree frogs and its bullfrogs, and with the smell of hibis-
cus and oleander, and with the balmy scents of the sea. Sardinia's
dry air slipped with us beneath the toasty sheets and blankets. It
was cool and quiet outside, and we curled on our beds with peace
in our hearts, with the sun still baking our skin, with the salt still
saturating our pores, with the memories of the slapping waves and
the hot fine sand and the jagged stones and pebbles still playing
our bodies' senses like an action film's soundtrack, protected by
our beds, and by the certainty of our adult parents returning home
soon, bringing safety with their casual clamor of jingling keys and
scraping shoes, slamming doors, and poorly suppressed whispers.
We forgot all about the jolts and jerks of the ashtray and its awful intimations, traded it for dreams of frosty seas and air mattress
battles, and for the glamorous body-surfing exploits we would un-
dertake the next day.

Fish Stew/Cassola

A fish stew from Sardegna is distinguished not so much by it's recipe but by its ocean dwelling ingredients, including, but not limited to gurnard, sea robin, eel, skate, bream, mullet, squid or octopus, scorpion fish, baby clams, and crabs. It is, along with cacciucco and cioppino, a fish stew that predates the French bouillabaisse by several centuries, and at the same time is, or can be, very similar. There are no fixed rules for this recipe, they vary widely, but one thing is clear. The base of this soup is fish stock made by hand. If that is done then everything else falls into place. This recipe is based on a Sardinian one, using fresh fish and shellfish more available in Eastern Europe and the USA.

To start:
24 clams, rinsed, brushed, and purged.
2 garlic cloves
2 tbsp olive oil
1 cup dry white wine

Put the clams in a sauté pan with the garlic and the oil. Heat the pan over medium heat till the oil is sizzling. Shake the pan to stir and turn clams. When garlic starts to soften, add wine and cover. Continue to shake pan gently. Let clams steam till they open. Discard clams that do not open, retain the rest. Save the pan juice.

Broth:
2 large fish heads, about two pounds (no salmon)
aromatics: 1 leek, sliced, 1 onion, sliced, 2 scallions, sliced, 3 cloves garlic, peeled and smashed, 1 bunch of parsley, 1 stalk celery, sliced. ALL aromatics should be thinly sliced.
1/2 cup dry white wine
retained clam pan juice from step 1.
peels from 700g shrimp
1 bay leaf
6 cups/1400 ml filtered water
1/8 tsp saffron threads

Place the oil and aromatics in a stockpot. Turn on the heat. Bring the oil to a sizzle and add fish heads and shrimp peels. Sauté with gentle stirring/folding for 10 minutes, until veggies are soft. Add white wine and allow deglazing and evaporating, about 3 minutes. Add water, reserved clam juice, bay leaf, and bring to a slow boil. Immediately turn to a simmer and reduce for about 20 minutes. Strain the broth gently into another stockpot and discard the solids. Add saffron threads and simmer, covered, for 10 minutes.

Preparing the Stew:

½ cup/120 ml Olive oil
1 roma tomato, finely diced
24 clams, reserved from step one.
700g shrimp meat, peeled and cleaned
2 pounds firm fleshed fish (grouper, cod, triggerfish, snapper, etc.)
450g squid bodies, cut into thin rings
2 lobster tails, boiled and thinly sliced
1 small can (5 oz/140g) tomato paste
1 onion, chopped
½ cup dry white wine
¼ tspn freshly ground Himalayan salt
freshly ground pepper to taste
1 tsp crushed red pepper
6 cloves garlic, peeled and smashed
½ cup chopped parsley
8 slices croutons (see note below)

Add oil, onions, garlic, red pepper and parsley to cold pan. Bring to a sauté. Let onion soften. Add the wine and simmer for about a minute. Add stock, parsley, tomatoes, tomato paste, and simmer for 20 minutes. Add fish and simmer till near done. Add shrimp and cook till almost pink. Add sliced lobster and clams and cook until warmed through. Serve in bowls lined with one or two croutons. Serves four.

Preparing the Croutons:

Preheat oven to 250 degrees. Slice Italian bread or baguette. Rub both sides with olive oil. Place in 250-degree oven till totally dry and hard, about 20 minutes. Remove from oven and let cool. Peel garlic cloves and rub them on both sides of the crusty bread. Put the bread in the bottom of the bowl, and pour the stew on top.

Remedy to keep witches from entering your home:

Set out a broom and a salt shaker outside your front door. The witches will have to count each grain of salt and each strand of the broom before they can enter your home, and if they make a mistake, they'll have to start over. If one manages to get in, cross your legs, and chant, "today it's Saturday at my house," as witches cannot travel abroad on Saturday.

A Kiss for Heaven's Sake

We always heard the siren after the planes were already rumbling above us. And the feeling that came with it—that was the worst of it. The bombings happened at all hours, but especially when we were asleep, tearing us from the only peace we knew, shaking us from our dreams and grabbing us by the throat to remind us of our misery. *Déh*! That sound entered our bones and plucked our spines like catgut. It was worse than the walls rendered to dust, worse than seeing pieces of people scattered all over town. When it came, we ran down the stairs in our bare feet and night robes and tried to keep quiet, which wasn't easy with the children and that awful siren wailing. The shelter was down the street. We crossed the porticos, hiding under the pillared airways, but after the porticos there was nothing above us but open sky.

My friend Rita whom I knew since first grade wore that long blue nightgown, so flimsy that when she ran it lifted up like bird feathers, and you could see the cotton hemline ripped from wash and wear. She wore flat black shoes, and on top of her blue gown, the sweater that her fiancé had given her. And of course there was that little gold bracelet, thin like a hair that she always had on her. She was so proud of that bracelet, turning it around her wrist when she spoke to you, beaming with that special glow of soon-to-be wives.

We were running, urging each other on, that siren wailing

louder and louder, and the roar of the planes vibrating inside our bellies. We pushed ahead, holding hands, shushing the children, corralling the little ones who wanted to go hide under a tree. The levanter wind stung our skin under our flimsy nightgowns. Rita's mom had already crossed the street, but the planes had swooped down just then, and Rita stepped back under the cover of the porticos, crying. Her mother cupped her lips to be heard above the roar. Who knows what she was trying to tell her? The siren was still wailing, but by then it wasn't helping. We couldn't hear our own thoughts.

The propeller planes dipped down, and all I heard then was that awful noise, rat,tat,tat,tat... and then screams and the hiss of the bombs falling, and then the explosions and that wailing siren making everything worse, and dust and shards flying at us from everywhere. And yet if you lifted your head, there was the moon, with her silvery shroud of cumulus, looking down at us as we bled, and I don't know why, but it made me think of God. The fire and the dust conspired with the mist, and we couldn't even figure out where the screams were coming from. Rita must have gotten scared and she'd hung back, and dear me, should I tell you this, but it was like the whole fleet of planes took it up against that one girl, made her the target of all their shooting as if she'd been single-handedly responsible for all the blood spilled in the war. The shots just kept coming, and she was crouched by that pillar, with her arms on her face, her hands stretched out, screaming, screaming, as if the air in her lungs could rescue her, d'eh!

"Cross over," her mother yelled, when the last plane lifted up.

"Come on Rita, quickly," I pleaded. I couldn't do anything but watch.

She stepped onto the street and then stepped back, crying "Mamma, mamma," while her mamma cried back, throwing her arm out telling her "Run, now, before the planes circle around and come back for us."

Nobody had the courage to run under the open sky to go get her.

By the time Rita got brave, one of the planes had already circled back and dipped down. I don't think I ever saw it, really. It was too dark, and there was too much smoke in the air, and still, I feel like I remember it, like I saw its snout, all glinting metal and spinning propeller. Pop, pop, pop, and Rita fell, just like that, not two steps from the porticos, her mother clawing her face and making a sound as if she were giving birth.

But in those days it was common to see things like this. It makes us feel bad now to talk about it, but every time someone died, we were glad it wasn't one of us. We were just a town of women, old men and children, but there was the steel mill up the Magona, and the planes came. They came for us day and night. Rita was the lucky one, and I'm not saying this for you to feel sorry for me: let me tell you about the grocer's wife, Alberta! Her son was only eleven years old. After the bombs fell and columns of smoke billowed up to the sky and there was nothing to do but to clear the rubble and bury the dead, I heard her voice tear up: "Somebody help me, please, somebody." But there was nobody who could help her. She had loaded her boy on a wheel barrow and she was pushing that wheel barrow down the road towards the hospital, her son spouting blood from a crack in his skull, his hair drenched wet, and his thin body limp like an old, rag doll. In that moment, I think I knew that the lucky ones are the dead. Grief is for the living. We are the ones who have to push our wheelbarrows down the road of our lives.

My cousin Marco, for example, right before he left for the war, he got engaged to this girl from the hills. Agnese. She had barely finished the third grade, and she couldn't read or write all that well. Her cursive was so bad that I had to be reading and writing the letters that this girl sent to the front. Agnese was a slip of a girl, chicken-boned, fragile and yellow like a tulip bud all wet with dew. She got sick with tuberculosis two years into the war, and the hunger didn't help, either. She withered up within weeks, but I kept writing love letters for her fiancé while Agnese dictated from bed. I did it because it helped me think about my Giorgio, who was out there with the Resistance, and God knew how much I wanted to know where he was. But it was dangerous in those days to know anything about the Partisans. The fascists came to our houses, searched our rooms, gutted even our pillows to find a letter. Where he was, I didn't want to know.

And so I wrote for Agnese, I wrote down to the moment when the girl gurgled in her own blood and let out the last breath like she had run a race to be with the Madonna and Jesus. I didn't know what to do. Marco was on the front fighting Russians. I'd heard of the things men had to suffer there, getting their hands cut off when the cold froze the blood and marching over the ice with broken shoes as if the bombs and the bayonets weren't hellish enough. I'd seen enough of them come back with those dead eyes, lice on their heads, an arm or a foot or a leg missing, and sparking like live wire when someone slammed a door or banged a pot. I didn't have the heart to write Marco that the love of his life had died. *Déh*! He wouldn't have been able to leave the front if he'd wanted to, anyway, and so, I kept on writing those letters, thinking I'd tell him face to face if he ever got to make it home.

It went on like that for a good while, until one day a letter came from Marco. He said, "I know she's dead because she came to me in my tent last night and she told me. She told me you're writing those letters for her and not to be angry with you because she knows you meant well, but stop it. I know how she died and when she died: it was over two months ago already. She went in her sleep. She told me that before she will go to heaven she wants me to kiss her one last time like I did when she was alive. Until then, she will wait for me."

Let me tell you, Bella, it was another two years before Marco came back to Piombino, *déh*. He was so gaunt you could count all his ribs even with his shirt on. He had that wild, faraway look of all our soldiers who came back, as if inside his head he was listening to the whistle of the bombs. *Déh*! You'd think by then, with all the death he'd seen the last thing he'd want was to see another dead person. But he had the body exhumed.

He'd look me dead in the eye with that dull stare of his, and he'd say, "Liliana, I told you. She asked me one thing, and one thing only. If it had been your Giorgio to ask you to do something, would you say no?"

Well, what could I tell him?

To have a grave dug out wasn't such an easy thing. First there was the municipal administrator to pay off, then the cemetery, and then of course the gravediggers. Even Padre Bonamanti wanted his share: because someone had to put Agnese back into the earth after Marco said goodbye, right? So the gravedigger arrived early in the morning, with that shovel over his shoulder, his cap lowered tight over his eyes. He didn't believe it, hardly, that he had to do this and he cursed Marco's ancestors all the way into the six feet of dirt he shoveled to get to her tomb, the dirt piling up in a mound behind him. He did it, though. There isn't much that a starving Christian won't do for a piece of bread.

All through the digging, my cousin Marco didn't budge. His face was drawn back on his bones so tight you could practically see his skull like it would look like after the worms got his last bit of flesh. His lips at the corners were tucked back in that frown.

I begged him not to do it. I said, "What do you want with the dead, eh? It was a dream, just a dream. This is sacrilegious, Marco."

Madonnina, did I beg him, with my hands together, praying to him.

Even Padre Bonamanti tried to talk him out of it. He said, "Son, your fiancé is with God, now. You will see her in heaven in the glory of the All Mighty."

But Marco wouldn't hear of it, his teeth clamping down on his cigarette, sucking up a drought of smoke for every curse the gravedigger threw back with shovelfuls of dirt. And I tell you that when that coffin was pried open, there she was, Agnese, as fresh as if she'd been buried only yesterday. It stunk of deep earth and stale air and wet wood, but she was whole, wearing the blue dress that she wore for her confirmation. Her arms were crossed over her breasts, and on her face, painted as if she'd been a Rafaelite Madonna, was that same pious smile she wore when Marco proposed to her.

Marco scooped her up. Just as soon as he lifted her, her torso broke at the waist with a little cracking sound, like her bones were made of cookies, but for the rest of her, believe me, she was still whole like she'd only just gone to sleep, a little jaundiced maybe, and thinner then she'd been when Marco used to bring her around for the dances in the Piazza, but there she was, with her lips just lightly parted, her thick black eyelashes resting on her cheeks, as though she'd been waiting for that kiss all those years.

Marco bent down and wrapped his arms around her and kissed her like she was still his, with the palm of his hand cradling the back of her head, her black hair still shiny and thick like it had been in life. "Rest, my dear," he told her, with his lips on her ear. He relaxed, then, for the first time since I'd seen him come home. You don't believe me, but Bella Mia, if I hadn't seen it with my own eyes I wouldn't have believed it myself. And then, the moment he put her down, she practically fell apart in a puff of dust. *Déh*!

The war. The war did such things to us, if only I could tell you half of them. When my Giorgio finally came home, he was a ghost of the man he'd been, the veins at his temples pushing up from under his skin like scars. For years he'd wake us all up cursing in German, screaming a high pitched cry and pointing at things that weren't there, swinging his head and rolling in bed trying to avoid the tanks in his head. I'd try to slip my arms through his flailing and hold him, and I'd cry, "Giorgio! Giorgio! You're home now." I'd get a sense, when I said it, of the improbability of what I was trying to tell him. Home? What is home? This squeaky bed? These cardboard walls? The walls weren't thick enough for the tanks in his head. But little by little he'd breathe a little softer and look at me.

You never survive a war, Cara Mia. So. It wasn't the tanks that took him. It wasn't the bullets of the Americans or the machine guns of the Germans. It wasn't even the cold or the famine, but God took him, everything of him except the body. God took the man, and I could only just have the shell, something to hold onto for my eyes to remember, just like Agnese in the grave, waiting for one last kiss before falling apart.

Pane dei Morti (Bread of the Dead)

Pane dei Morti is a cross between a fruitcake and a hearty cookie. It is a traditional food that many associate with Halloween, but is actually prepared for All Souls Day, November 1st, when Italians remember and pay respect to their ancestors. You will find this on bakers' shelves for the first week of November only, after which they disappear until the following year. As with most Italian recipes, there are dozens of variations based on region and family.

100g dried figs, finely chopped
100g raisins
25g candied orange peel
25g candied lemon peel
150g macaroons
150g Biscoff cookies
200g savoiardi (ladyfingers)
300g sugar
50g sweet marsala wine
50 grams cognac or brandy
120g hazelnut grain
250g tipo 00 flour
6 egg whites
1 tsp cinnamon
pinch grated nutmeg
½ package dry yeast
10g baking powder

Place the raisins and chopped figs in lukewarm water to reconstitute. Place Biscoff, macaroons, hazelnuts, and ladyfingers into a food processor and process to crumbles. Pour into a bowl.

Add flour, cocoa, nutmeg, sugar, and cinnamon to chopped cookies. Squeeze water out of figs and raisins, add to bowl. Add candied citrus rinds. Add yeast, baking powder, cognac, marsala, and egg whites. Mix and knead till dough is well mixed and smooth. Form it into a loaf and cut and mold the dough into biscotti size shapes. Put on a baking dish covered with parchment, place in a preheated 180 degree oven, and bake for 25 minutes.

Remove from oven, sprinkle with powdered sugar, let relax. Cookies should sit covered for a couple of days in an idle oven before serving.

Remedy against ghosts:

To keep a house clean of malignant ghosts, one must hammer a nail in their front door: to have effect against ghosts, the nail must come from a casket. However, finding a nail in the streets on the first day of the year is good luck, and hammering it to a kitchen door enhances good fortune.

Shot

You were always too slow, your father used to say, too slow dodging the other girls' hands blocking your shots, slow to move out of the way, slow to catch up, slow to make the basket -- just like when you were ten, at ski camp, he'd remind you, where you were sent in hopes you'd learn some self-preservation skills, hopes all but lost the day of the storm when the competition was canceled, but somehow you had already gotten to the top of the mountain, early as your father had suggested, so you could study the slope alone, testing the ice, the snow, the binding of your skis, you, still struggling with your gear and missing the last lift down, and slow to bundle up with adequate scarves and gloves, slow to apprehend the context of the warning passing around from mouth to mouth, missed everything important; and although you hardly talk to your father anymore now that you're earning your own money, he'll still have seen you today, maybe from the bleachers, maybe in his mind, still thinking you're always one second or so too late to shoot, too slow to move out of the way for the referee to call a foul he's not sure he's seen, too slow telling the coach how the girl with the frizzy hair slugged you one under your chin so that you got confused and didn't know where you were, and the game turned into a stampede of squeaking sneakers, flying sweat, and shoving hands, and wouldn't slow down for you, (although it didn't seem like such a long time to you) and you just stood there under a rain of whistles and shouts, costing your team two points, slow like molasses as they say in the South, but not quite that sweet because you're too slow with a compliment from the boy who, after the game, told you that referee was crazy not to call that foul, and that your shots seemed elegant from where he sat, high up on the bleachers, and in spite of yourself, you have difficulties processing how there might be some things about you that are elegant, after all, and you fail to show interest or gratitude for this person whose smile is better than one hundred foul shots from the foul line where no one can trample you, better even than that invitation to the party tonight he's just offered, where the coach has agreed the team should go to celebrate - but even in the comfort of beer and dim lights you're too slow to prevent the girl with the frizzy hair and big breasts who slugged you one on the basketball court earlier today from moving in on the kill before you, slow on the dance floor, slow to think of how to react to the way he looks at you as she takes his hand and leads him away, her teeth showing, her breasts rubbing against his chest as she nudges him to a cozy corner behind the beer keg where their bodies merge to the mellifluous tones of a Latin ballad, where you know now it's too late for you to go, too late to answer his subtle invitation, too late for a fair score, too late to catch the last ride home, like that day at ski camp, when you felt too numb with fear of losing to see the snow storm coming, the wind rising up fast all around you and the fog swallowing you quickly, quickly, until the rescue team had to be sent to find you, you, the slow one, hunched down against the fast wind, inching your way down the slope through feet of powder-fresh snow, still thinking about winning, your fingers and toes frosting one by one, your tongue tasting metal, until the arm of someone you couldn't see wrapped around you, snow and cold tufts of steamy breath congealing on your ski mask as he spoke to you of safety, of shelters, of canceled competitions; even now, with your arms wrapped around you in a sober hug while a slow song plays out, you remember how it felt to be rescued, to know the slow beat of a stranger's breath catching up to your quick gasps: because you know you will have to get home tonight somehow, but an arm may yet reach out and wrap around you, the arm of a stranger who won't ask for your name, or ask what you're doing here alone tonight in this dangerous darkness, won't ask how you expect to get safely to a warm, slow place you call home that you would otherwise have to earn walking alone from glower, to yowl, to whispered propositions of strangers leaning in the shadows of corners, offering sex, offering drugs, offering slow and dreamy dissolutions for a price, and you making your way through these streets alone, will pretend not to see them, as if it weren't urgent, as if it weren't all about living or dying, as if happiness were all just a whistle away from that elegant shot you took after the party on an empty court, no one watching, no one missing it, no one to evaluate how elegant it seemed, and no one to criticize you, like your father used to, for taking your time.

Lemon Granita Float

On hot Italian summers, many sidewalk cafes will offer ample selections of granita drinks: crushed ice infused with flavored fruit syrup occasionally spiced with a shot of liquor. Granita is the precursor of the Italian ice.

2 cups Water
2 cups evaporated cane sugar
1 cup lemon juice
1 tbsp lemon zest
1 shot Prosecco
1 shot vodka, kept in freezer
1 shot limoncello, kept in freezer
a sprig of mint leaves, bruised

Gently boil the water and sugar till sugar is just dissolved. Let cool. Add lemon juice and zest (no white pith) to syrup. Poor into a 9x13" metal baking pan with raised sides. Place in freezer for 20 minutes. Scrape granita with a spatula up from the bottom and sides of the pan. Place back in freezer and scrape again in 20 minutes. Repeat till all the syrup has frozen and the granita is grainy but not hard ice.

Place one shot each of Prosecco, vodka, and limoncello in a champagne flute. Carefully float a scoop of granita into the flute. Garnish with a bruised mint leaf. Serve immediately.

Remedy to gain the love of someone you desire:

On a Monday on a full moon, gather some dew drops or some holy water. Drop and mix the holy water or dew in the wine or water of the loved one to drink. For a woman who desires a man, mixing a few drops of her menstrual blood in the food she must cook and serve for him will bind the man's heart to her for life if he eats it.

Nonna

Nonna's real name is Lily, a fragrant flower, a sweet intoxication of yellows, but the children know her only as the Nonna who every winter rides the train from Piombino to Livorno, from Livorno to Milan, clutching a hard-skinned suitcase the color of grief that bumps against her weak knee while the yellows of her paisley dress twine about her large girth. Nonna of the light step, of the vigor in the laughter, Nonna at the door, wrapped in a rush of hugs, a chiming of joyful cries. Nonna's arms are strong as they receive the tumble of children, who crawl under her legs, who want to hold on to her calves and ask her to bake crunchy chiacchere cookies all powdered up like brides. They cry, Nonna, we're so glad you've come, and they stumble over her large suitcase to see what gifts she's brought, dolls stitched in fabric and wool, stickers with butterflies and flowers, swirling lollipops stuffed inside socks so they won't break with the hardship of travel. Nonna of the flour smells; Nonna of the romps and pillow fights.

Nonna is in the bathroom of the Milan condo, smoking a cigarette, laughing through the gap in her front teeth as she hunkers against the humid cold. The children pull on the door handle, tinker with the skeleton key. Where are you? Nonna cara, carissima nonna, nonnanonnanonnina. Nonna sits on the toilet, blowing smoke rings out the crack of an opened window; she watches a yellow flowered curtain flutter in the toxic Milan wind. Tuscan sausages and wild boar are tucked in her suitcase in thin paper, a taste of home for her daughter. When the children laugh through the keyhole, she cups her hand to her ear like a seashell to funnel the low murmur of the ocean in her breath.

Nonna feels out of context in Milan. She locks the double bolted doors when the children go to kindergarten. She waits in the kitchen where her fingers play with egg and flour, where her flat thumbnails push cheese inside pillows of dough, Nonna of the spicy rabbit sauce and the baked chestnut bread. Her visits are flavored with black pepper and rosemary. Her daughter sits on a high stool in the kitchen, cutting squares from rolled dough, hinting to plans for another move. Where to? Asks Nonna. She pretends not to see when her daughter looks out the yellow flowers curtains to the smog-grimy street. Every winter her son in law's job pushes them a little farther, migrations that translate to compartments in the bruised violet suitcase now gaping open at the foot of the trundle bed in the studio. The suitcase sighs an odor like family, salami, lollipop, sausage and dried porcini mushroom, socks that smell like caciotta cheese, blouses worn once, carrying the scent of salt, low-heeled shoes smeared with the moss of the beach and rocks below her house, the crushed pack of cigarettes she inhales like unanswered prayers.

Nonna talks to the neighbors from the window of her third floor apartment, chats through the cry of gulls and the roar of mopeds, looking out for that car with the Milan tag, packed and full of children. Nonna's feet are always sandy and mucked with beach petroleum, Nonna who knows to bring peach nectar and prosciutto sandwiches to coax the kids out of the water when their fingers wilt with salt and sea. Summers last one week, a weekend, a day or two on the way to the new beach house in Sardinia. When the kids pack up after summer is over, Nonna offers them five hundred liras each. The youngest child cries. Are you sad because you won't see your Nonna until next year? He holds up his five hundred liras with two fingers and rubs his wet nose, says, This, I don't know.

Nonna receives the news that her daughter will be moving to New York, America, through a long-distance phone call. Nonna has a picture of her husband on the chest of drawers in the bedroom, the only picture that survived the bombs while she hid in the hills on her grandfather's farm. Now in the afternoon shadow of this two-room apartment, her husband smiles with the perpetual expectation of a future that never comes. One by one, the children get on the phone: Nonnina, how are you? Nonna's knee joints are bad, but she keeps this to herself. She wants to tell the kids about the war, about the years of love the Fascists stole from her. Her daughter gets on the phone, says Mamma, this is too much. Hang up, already. Do you want to bankrupt yourself? Wait until Easter. You'll have time to tell these things. Nonna is always waiting for something, to be of age for the dance, to be old enough to stop sneaking kisses under the bales of hay, to be pretty enough for marriage. She waits for Fascism to end, for the midnight incursions to stop, mattresses gutted, drawers smashed, her husband hiding in a ditch in the woods, the war, the Russian steppes in winter, and the letters that come always too late, and then finally when it seems all is over, waiting again for the neighbors to tell her the truth about the so-called accident, and for her daughter to grow up without a father, and for herself, to understand what all the crying was for, and for God to remember she's still here. A pot of lumachini snails boils on the stove. Nonna cleans tripe in the sink, sets up the couch with crisp sheets that smell like chef's soap. She is always happy to see them, no matter how many years pass between each visit. What year are you in school? What are you studying in history class? Her sentences tumble over each other like a game of leapfrog. At night before bedtime, she retells all the fairytales with comical endings, adorns the punch lines with pretend farts and blames the mopeds, brays her laughter louder than the kids. She is Nonna of the blue hair. She is Nonna of the wide-gapped teeth. She is Nonna of the flat shoes and wide girth.

Nonna's breath grows thick as she climbs up to the third floor, Nonna who gives the children five thousand of the old liras not knowing the currency has changed while the money waited in a jar. Her doctor found a murmur in her heart. She likes the sound of this illness: a murmur, a whisper, a burbling of friendly ghosts calling to her, the Lily, the intoxications of youth, her husband in a soldier's uniform calling at the door. Nonna checks New York crime statistics in the newspaper. On the phone, she says, Keep the children safe. This is Nonna trying to have a conversation through the long distance beeping of satellites, the echoing of voices like murmurs from the beyond, her daughter floating as distantly as the orbit of a satellite.

It has been years now since anyone has called her Lily. She is no longer Lily, but Nonna of the packing suitcases, Nonna of the cardboard boxes empty and gaping open, scattered on the living room floor, Nonna with the American daughter full with ambition enough to try to dig up a wilted Lily and plant her in New York. Nonna of the now small girth and heavy step, trembles as she climbs the third floor steps, a thin plastic shopping bag bumping against her bad knee straining from too much weight, stretching and thinning from her grip, that window overlooking the beach waiting behind a closed door, atop three more steps, the view of brambles and rocks, the relentless beating of the waves below crowding in her chest. She's allergic to aspirin, to penicillin, to ibuprofen; her breath labors through the gap in her front teeth. The murmur in her heart says America is just another dream; she will forever be the Nonna of the Tuscan hills, of the chestnut bread and pillows of dough.

She reclines against the hospital bed, unable to remember how she got here from Piombino to Livorno, from Livorno to this hospital, covered in this gown the color of virgins, and the neighbor who now holds her hand, calls her by her name, tells her that her daughter is on her way from New York. Lily. Lily. The name doesn't sound right. Nonna waits. She is Nonna of the nine hours flight from America, Nonna of the two-hour train ride from Milan, Nonna of the mistral wind blowing over the sea, Nonna of the light breath, of the powdered sugars, of the breathings of greetings, Nonna of the Milan Christmases, of the Tuscan summers, of the olives, the chestnuts, the cypress trees, Nonna, a rhyme from a fairy tale, a scent like flour and cigarettes, a jingle of coins in a jar, a sudden fragrance of lilies, an exhalation of the sea, a murmur in the heart...

Chiacchiere

Chiacchiere means "gossip," or "chatter." These sweet treats also known as "fiocchi" (ribbons) or "cenci" (rags), are, literally, ribbons of fried dough, similar to funnel cakes, but cooked to be crispier. Chiacchiere are traditionally eaten during Carneval, the celebration of Fat Tuesday that begins the period of Lenten fasting in the Catholic church.

450g all-purpose flour
4 tbsp unsalted butter, softened
2/3 cup confectioners sugar
2 tbsp baking powder
4 eggs
1 tbsp brandy
1 tbsp sweet marsala wine
½ tbsp vanilla
1 tbsp lemon juice
1 tbsp lemon zest
a pinch of Himalayan salt
flavorful oil for frying (beef tallow, lard, or unrefined peanut oil at 350 degrees)

Mix all the ingredients together, incorporate well and knead for 10 minutes or so, until you have smooth, dry, stiff dough. If too wet, add flour. Wrap tightly and let it sit for about an hour.

Using a pasta machine, roll an orange-sized piece of dough to the width of a pie crust, fold several times and roll it out again to pie crust thickness. Cut the dough into 50x125 mm strips (roughly 2x5 inches). Slice a 3 inch slit in the center of each strip. Gently bring one end of the dough through the slit and lay flat. This is called a lover's knot.

Fry in batches for 2-3 minutes, until lightly browned. Drain on paper towels, dust well with confectioners sugar when cooled.

Remedy to ensure future love and happiness for a newborn baby girl:
Soon after the baby girl is born, powder her up with sugar between her thighs. When she grows up, she will attract many suitors, and she will marry well and early.

Cold War

The boy I fell in love with was waiting outside my favorite diner in a jacket too thin for the cold. I was thirty, available, and always on a diet, and therefore, irrational as that may sound, I was a regular at this diner. I went for banana-strawberry whole-wheat pancakes, which sounds worse than it is. Brian had seen me before, once, with a group of nice kids from the Iowa Workshop. I remembered his name because he'd taken our orders, and when we told him we were students in the Workshop, he'd tried to make us believe that the diner was haunted, sounding much like a liar until he confessed that he was trying to impress us. But today I was alone, and Brian, even though he barely knew me, gave me a nod like he had been suffering the cold waiting just for me.

He held the doors of the diner open, letting all that warm steam flow out and I said, "No, I have to buy a paper, first," shaking the coins in my fist. Brian jammed a cigarette between his teeth and kicked the door farther open, then, balancing on his other leg, he leaned forward and dropped a quarter in the newspaper dispenser, his body posed like the flying warrior asana in yoga, balancing one leg straight back, stretching his arms out in front of him. I said thank you. I was impressed. I grabbed my paper.

"Get me one too," he said, his lips still tightly wrapped around that cigarette he'd been trying to light up before I got there. He waited until I slipped past him, out of the cold; then he walked in after me, waved me towards a booth, and while I settled in, he grabbed the coffee pot and a mug. He placed the napkin-wrapped silverware in front of me and sat down across from me, his arms folded.

"So," he said. "You look exotic. Where are you from?"

Now, the only thing exotic about me was that my blond hair was died and not natural, which, granted, in Iowa was a little un- usual, but he said, "You know, I get you. I'm, like, the only black guy in this town," which wasn't true, but I knew what he meant. Before I moved here from Florida my friend had warned, "In Iowa, even the black people are white," and then he and his girlfriend had snickered like this was a joke between them. Brian waved at some- body in the doorway, an elder gentleman followed by two young boys, and before I could say a word, he got up, taking his coffee pot, and said, "You weren't shittin' me that day. You're really with the Writers' Workshop?"

"Hmm," I hummed noncommittally. The locals made a big fuss about the Workshop, maybe because it was their claim to fame for a prairie, Midwestern town that would otherwise be known only for its pooping pig souvenir dolls and its football team, but I didn't feel like such a big deal. All I had to show for my talent, besides my acceptance here, was a stack of pre-formatted rejection letters of editors who told me, in the nicest possible way, that they didn't like my writing.

Brian wagged a finger at me. "I wrote some stories I want to show you."

I gave him a fake smile, hoping to telegraph my lack of enthu- siasm, and began to pay careful scrutiny to the menu. Every time I told some perfect stranger that I was trying to become a writer, I had to talk my way out of having to line edit a seven-hundred-page tome. *It will make us both rich. You won't be sorry, I promise.* Ok.

I was a teaching assistant, for god's sake, a synonym for mi- grant laborer, and I had freshmen papers to grade, a whole stack

of them. I had counted on occupying this one booth until din-
nertime, until they kicked me out, until I got through half of my
papers and had to go somewhere else for a warm place to work.
My apartment on the upper floor of an old Victorian had chinks
and cracks so wide a squirrel could have squeezed through them.
Every time I tried to turn on my electric heater I'd short circuit the
house with a spark and a pop. There weren't enough blankets in the
Midwest to stop me from shivering. The only warm place in town
was this diner.

Brian came back to the booth with my pancakes, which had a
smile shaped out of pieces of strawberries and bananas.

"I made it for you," he informed me, admiring his own creation.

"It's cute."

"We make this for the children on Sundays. I was practicing."

I pulled out my freshmen rhetoric papers and my red pen.

"You shouldn't use a red pen, you know?" Brian said. "I can
get you a green pen from the office." He looked over my shoulder.
"C? You're giving that guy a C?" He took the pen from my hands
and bubbled in a B in place of the C. "That's better," he said. He
blinked at me. I think I blinked at him. "Aren't you annoyed with
me yet?"

I should've said, "Quite." I should've said, "Please leave me
alone: I need to work," but I just wasn't raised that way. My mother is a small-town Italian. In small-town Italy people are greatly
concerned with manners, much more then they're concerned with
drawing boundaries. I shook my head, no.

"I'll keep trying," he said.

It was 2002 and the world had fallen around me barely a few
months before. After class, my workshop peers and I ambled
through the snow to the local pub, where we watched tanks explode on muted television sets, with classic rock blasting and competing against the clinking of beer glasses.

"So what you're saying," said an obnoxious school mate sitting in front of me, "is that if it weren't for reputations, you'd sleep with any guy who'd ask you."

"No. What I'm saying," I clarified, "is that women have the same sexual urges as men. If we learned to suppress them it's because of nurture, not because of nature."

"But you women have standards," said another guy. "We go through the good looking women first, but we look at the uglies and we say, hey, just wait, fatty: we'll get to you, too." He nodded at a fat middle-aged woman at the bar, taking a sip of his beer.

I forgot to laugh. My eyes traveled to the surreal distance of the orange clouds of desert dust and fire on TV. In a town snowed in on all borders from miles of pig farms, we could get pretty claustrophobic, gossip revolving around the same parties, thrown by the same people, or about the stench of dung that pervaded the town on days when farmers fertilized. It felt to me then that our small town unimportance was now being tallied against the enormity of a world event most of us could not begin to fathom.

Being a middle-aged grad student in a mid-western town while your country is attempting to organize for war against an invisible enemy can be unsettling. The Government was trying to cross t's by prohibiting plastic knives on international flights. We were meeting in bars, still trying to talk about sex.

"Maybe we should do something about this," I said, nodding at the television while it was on a commercial break. The one who'd winked at the fat woman turned to observe the muted television: two identical polo shirts suffered ketchup squirts, which were promptly doused with blue laundry detergent.

"We could draft an anti-war statement or something," I clarified.

"Don't change the subject," said the obnoxious one, pointing a finger at the low cut of my shirt. "You said you'd fuck any guy."

A few days later we had a meeting. We quickly fell into disorganized discussion, some taking sides with Our President, others pontificating on the subtler points of a democracy under threat. Already then we had cut the Bush jokes. Even the staunchest liberals were referring to Mr. Bush as "Our President" with a ring of solemnity that measured up to a church vow.

"Hey!" I shouted above the din. "I think this thing about becoming allies with Pakistan is a mistake. Awful. Who thought of that one? And why! It will backfire."

"I don't know," a friend said, thoughtfully. "I just don't know. War seems...it seems like I should trust my President on this."

We left the meeting feeling more deflated than before, hungry for news and finding the news stands looted by med students willing to get up earlier than writers. The only news we shared was of so and so or such and such who went back to New York, who lost an uncle, a boyfriend, a cousin, and who might not be back next semester.

I did what any Catholic, single Italian thirty year old would do in my shoes: I went to church. There were people, there was singing, and we held hands and knew all the hymns and smiled and looked forward to something.

I liked that church. The priest kept his sermons short and the list of anonymous prayer request long and full of details, and on Sundays, hope brimmed as we lifted our hearts to the Lord and offered them up like the innocent lambs we all hoped we still were, in spite of Osama Bin Laden's terrifying perversity. This spell lasted an hour; then it was time to be lonely again, cold, and confused while the country was busily and purposefully at war. At the end of mass, I winced when I heard my anonymous prayer requests, written in the third person, warped by the priest's voice: "Pray for Laura who....wants...and .... I can't read this. Lord, grant her prayer. Go in peace."

Laura wanted a clue from the Divine; more than that, she wanted a partner in love, someone to go through the Apocalypse with her; someone to hold at night while smart missiles explode into granite Afghani caves. I prayed to find someone to share my Sunday pancakes with me, while Afghani children gathered under parachutes of US care packs, praying to Allah for the packages not to be bombs. Judgment Day, I was sure, would be more bearable with a partner. Dear Madonna, is it so much to ask? I said a rosary every night. To be thirty was acceptable; even to be in school and unemployed, but not to be alone, so hungry, dear Lord, so cold.

I bought a pretty spell book with a blood-red fabric cover, a look of old witch magic about it. It said something about burying a love wish in the earth bed of a budding rose, and I went to the organic co-op to plant my wish into the redolent brown earth of a potted rose. That is how I'd slipped, ever so dreamily, into witchcraft. Since childhood, my nonna had taught me to shell beans to predict the number of children I would one day have, to slip a potato under my pillow to dream the name of my future husband, to match dreams with numbers to play in the lottery, and to read the lines in my palms for clues of the future: all while lighting votives to the Madonna, and reading special prayers to St. Jude, who makes the impossible possible. It was no big deal, once in a while, to go that extra length for a wish. With the Lord's prayer, and the Madonna's blessing, a little magic is excused.

And when Brian sat before me, again, at that same booth a month later, I had already finished my tempe burrito, the only full meal I'd allow myself to eat for the day. I was picking at cold fries and going through my last folder of freshmen Rhetoric. He had been filling my coffee cup for hours. He hadn't asked me once yet if I wanted the check. He said, "I write children's stories. Would you have a look at them sometime?"

Brian slipped the ketchup bottle in his coat pocket and an unlit cigarette in his mouth, until I nodded in assent. He waited, straight face, for me to stop giggling. Then he got up, and bussed a few tables. I'd almost forgotten about his request when he came back and dumped a stack of hundreds of pages where my plate had just been. He offered a pot of fresh-brewed coffee. I had already drunk past the bladder test, but I accepted the payment. "All this, huh?" I adjusted the pages.

"I'll be back later," Brian said, suddenly shy.

I figured I had two choices: I could slip out the back door and never come back to this, my favorite diner, or suck it up and immerse myself in Brian's books.

When Brian came back, I gave him my critical review, pointing out the lines that needed more clarity, the paragraphs that needed development.

"What are you doing tonight?" Brian interrupted me. "Wanna have dinner?"

I looked at him, stunned to silence. I evaluated the situation. Me: a white Catholic Italian who loves her outdated, old-fashioned parents very much. Brian: a stick-thin, hip sort of guy a few years younger than me, and of African American descent. These were ingredients for the kind of relationship my parents would not accept without a tragedy of Puccinian proportions: "What will the family back home say about your being with a black guy!!!!" I would have braved this kind of tragedy for a *Princess' Bride* kind of true love, but I had to measure carefully if this guy sitting in front of me, with those thrift-store clothes and pierced nose, this guy who talked to me (and to everyone who came in the diner) as if he'd known us since kindergarten, I had to consider if he was the kind of person to fall in love with a thirty year old, seriously minded Italian woman looking for true love. The answer, I could see right there, was no. But somehow I said yes. I said sure. I said why not, I'm not doing anything.

I could blame it on my wish in the potted rose, I could blame it on the Catholic promises of a Madonna who forgives cheap spells, or I could blame it on the practiced way that Brian had planned out our evening on that unusually mild Iowa April night, waiting for the restaurant to close down, then cooking me Buddhist delight, just me and him in that cavernous candle-lit diner, the sound track of the Virgin Suicides playing on the speaker system. I could blame it on a lot of things, but mostly people do stupid things because they're brought to the point where it is either the stupid thing or spending the night in a cold home, eating bread cooked unevenly from an old gas stove and trying to get warm by breathing under blankets.

A few evenings later, our bodies were naked and tangled together in my living room's futon. A pink sunset light streaked through the hastily lowered blinds. I'd barely moved to reach for my bra when Brian said, "Do you know Tiffany Blue?"

"Doesn't sound familiar," I said, stroking his legs.

"She's in the workshop." He sat up as if annoyed.

I shrugged. "She must be a poet."

He reached for a cigarette, an eyebrow raised. He's slipped his glasses back on and he studied me as if I were trying to pull one over him. "How do you know?"

"Because poets never hang out with fiction writers around here. We even go to different bars."

He made a strange hissing sound, shook his head, said, "You snobs."

I couldn't disagree, but I had come to Iowa when the rules were already standing. I had never been good at popularity: I just went where my workshop peers went.

"I'm in love with her," he announced. The words came so suddenly, so earnestly, that I thought I had misheard him.

"What?" I covered my breasts; I reached for my shirt.

"I am so in love with her, whenever I see her I just want to kiss her. Oh, and I'm going out with this other woman, Pat, you know her?" He sucked on his cigarette, exhaled loudly, then: "She has this little girl. I love that child. I'm not sure if I'm in love with Pat or with that child. I have a daughter, too. But when Pat looks at me...I never had anyone look at me like that."

There was more: he was married. He was a recovering alcoholic. He was separated but he wanted to be supported by a rich woman.

Then he said, "Thank you for being so nice to me," as if rather then sleeping with him I'd given him a haircut.

He was in his socks and underwear, sitting on the edge of the futon, smiling at me, his fingers still tracing the curve of my inner thigh. I kicked him until he fell over the side. He looked down at my leg like it had malfunctioned.

"But you're leaving for Florida," he cried, his clothes clutched to his chest. "I didn't think you'd care. You're leaving in, like, days!"

"Get out of my house," I said, for lack of experience, impersonating one of those gorgeous Hollywood women who can shove a beautiful man out the door because she can expect him to come back at some point, changed and repentant, with a wedding ring in his hands.

By mercy, graduation time rolled around fast, and my sister came to visit from Rome, and I went with her to Chicago, and later we drove around Iowa, seeing nothing but farmlands, ducks, rabbits and assorted birds whose species we did not know. We caught up on gossip about our relatives in the old country, skipping Brian, skipping my loneliness, skipping my addiction to banana pancakes and my obsession with BMI. Next to her, I didn't have to be in Brian's body, smelling his sweat, feeling the soft lips drink dreams from mine.

But Vittoria went home to Italy, and I went back to my cold, cold house, two pounds heavier with Chicago-style pizza, and when Brian called, I answered the phone, maybe hoping the tenor tones of his voice would warm me.

"I woke up this morning in this hospital," he said, by way of a greeting. "I don't know how I got here, but I have slash marks on my wrist." After a short pause he said, "All I could think about was you, how nice you were to me. All I wanted to do was to hear your voice."

As an industrial-age baby, I was vaccinated against the deadliest of diseases; as a middle-class teen, I was saved from terminal poverty through education; but somehow through my few disastrous relationships I was still vulnerable to the obvious dangers of a few kind words spoken with temporary sincerity.

When Brian hung up, I bent under the bed and slid out a box

with all the newspapers I had collected since September 11th. I spread the clips out on the wood floors. I was supposed to pack my things, make arrangements for ending my lease, confirm my arrival to my tenant in Florida, and most of all, get all the paperwork signed for my graduation, but instead I made a carpet of news right there on the floor, the photographs of Iraqis, Afghanis and Pakistanis lying in the distilled perfection of a captured moment, the faces of protesters and victims staring up towards me as I sometimes stared at the ceiling of a cathedral, without much expectations or distraction from the drama surrounding me, but still, all the same, looking up.

What I had been saving these newspapers for, I wasn't sure: a moment when everything would come together and make sense, a moment where we could gather all the pieces and begin again, but the number of papers folded under my bed had turned into a small pile, and things didn't seem any clearer than they had on September 11th.

I got out my scissors and I cut out the pictures I liked best: the mountains of Afghanistan in the backdrop of a perfect sunset; Pakistani soldiers kicking protesters in the head, their muscled legs stretching high in ballet-like poses; the gigantic carving of Buddhas just before the Taliban exploded them, confirming the impermanence the Buddha had warned us about; Americans in spacesuits storming a post office contaminated by anthrax; families of the victims of the World Trade Center holding hands at a memorial. I glued them on poster paper of a color like skin, and I collaged the pictures together without any pattern other than their hues and shapes and framed the whole thing in Plexiglass.

When others saw it, they didn't ask what it meant or what it was. They only asked, "Who made this?" and I knew, by how their eyelids wrapped tightly around their eyes, that they understood.

When my lease was up, and all my possessions packed in my station wagon so that only the driver seat was free, Brian asked me to move in with him. Like the Buddha, we never talked about permanence: he had a court order to get sober and thanks to some strings pulled by his lawyer brother, he'd gotten into a famous rehab program in Minnesota. Still we kept postponing our departures with those casual phrases that experienced lovers know how to exchange through mundane guises of coffee cups and laundry piles. Just one more day. Because I needed an oil change. Because Brian's lease wasn't up until next month and it was already paid for.

A few days of breathing on Brian's skin turned into a few weeks of clothing myself from the suitcase in the backseat of my car. We ate in restaurants that served organic foods, and drank virgin Bloody Mary's, and Brian talked to strangers at nearby tables invading their privacy like a reality show host to offer unsolicited advice. We watched Iowa explode with red buds and dogwoods in the warm breath of late spring. He wasn't drinking, and I wasn't eating, but we romanced ourselves on the sidewalk in quaint downtown café's. We bought sandwiches that we couldn't finish because of my permanent diet, and because Brian was too impatient to stay put. If the homeless guy was around, begging a cigarette from table to table, Brian would call him out by his first name, slap him high-fives, and devise stratagems to offer away his leftovers.

"It's just a shame to throw all this good food away; I'd take it home, but we don't have a fridge, so it's just going to spoil."

I was proud of Brian, proud that he thought enough of this stranger to pretend it wasn't charity.

"Well, if you're not going to eat it…I'll take it off your hands."

It was Brian's mission to feed the world, whether the world was hungry or just in need of a light snack. We crashed frat parties and the get-togethers just to sneak into the kitchens of strangers to bake zucchini bread or sprinkle peanuts over pad thai. I was his lookout. If someone got near, I was supposed to distract them by standing sexily against the doorpost, making love to a beer bottle with my lips and start up a conversation. We stayed only for as long as it took for Brian to set up his dishes in saucy swirls and leafy apostrophes, then we'd leave the party without taking a single bite.

And I was swept away by the surreptitious gift giving, not realizing that crashing people's lives and leaving without a trace was what Brian did best.

"But when? When exactly are you coming home?" My father's voice on the phone had raised a pitch and I could tell that he suspected something. Now the third degree would begin: "What's wrong with your car."

"I don't know exactly. They said...the brake pads."

"The brake pads? And it takes a whole week to replace some brake pads?"

"I don't know, Dad, I don't know. Maybe there's something else wrong. Maybe they're taking advantage."

Long sigh. "So when? The week after?"

"Maybe the week after," Brian looked at me, with a hand on the counter, his glasses slipping a little from his long nose. "Or... whenever I fix this problem with the graduation certificate. I would rather do it now that I'm here then wait when I'm back in Florida."

"So, where are you living now?"

"With a friend."

"What friend?"

"Just a friend. It's a name to you, what do you care? You don't know anybody here."

Brian paced around the kitchen, pulling long drags from his cigarette, opening the coffee can and sealing it again. He banged a teaspoon against the coffee mug, then slammed the cabinet door.

When I hung up, he offered a mock expression of hurt.

"You should've told him you met someone special."

"Am I special to you now?"

All my high-school social disasters crashed over my head, staining my face with all sorts of ugly expressions. We both looked away.

One morning, as I woke up, I found Brian looking at me.

I smiled at him, purring like a cat. "Good morning, sunshine."

"I'll tell you something we say about white people," he said.

"When white people are wet, they smell funny. Sometimes we go in a subway car or something, and there's a wet white guy, and we brothers look at each other like... what the hell?"

"Are you trying to tell me something?" I snapped, gathering the blankets around me. "Do I smell? Is that it?"

"I'm giving you an in. I'm telling you something most people don't know."

"Are you seriously expecting me *not* to get offended?"

I stomped off with a pillow stuck to my chest, heading for the shower, banging things around too gently not to hear Brian sigh his, "White people..."

That was the day it began, White People, White People, and I didn't make the connection to my father's call for a long time, not even when I'd say, "But hey, I'm white people," and he'd sigh like I'd just tried to ride a bicycle for the first time and ended with my face in the dirt.

"When I say White People, I don't mean a specific person." And then he said, "There are certain kinds of black people I don't really get along with, either."

The war was on and it was just a matter of time, which one of us would pack it first. Tension lived in my mouth, on my tongue, on my clothes and in my past. I had to re-examine everything with Brian's eyes, my best friends in high-school, my disgust with women who wear veils, the country club my parents belonged to and where they forced me to spend my summers even though the other kids would follow me, singing "I like to live in America," because my injury at their mistaking my ethnicity contained a seed of dirty, embarrassing wrongness... There wasn't anything I could touch that wouldn't explode with an accusation: I was White People.

We ambled home from the cafe' where I maxed out my credit card to feed him. We saw a girl walking fast with her head straight, a convertible following her slowly, the window rolled down, the man in the driver's seat saying, "Get in. Get back in the car."

I said, "He should get out of the car and apologize. Why don't guys ever learn?"

Brian rolled his eyes. "When will women ever learn that guys cheat?"

Around that time, he began to leave poems for me to find, on the refrigerator, or on my computer screen, coded notes of his mixed feelings.

Arched above your mouth,
I plunge into your unspoken.
I feed you our daily hurt.

The body does not hide
digging trenches for its wars.
I offer out to sacrifice
the shivering of sex.

Then one afternoon, he got out of bed, and still naked, looked into my closet, moving the perches around.
"Do you have a dress I could borrow?"
I still smelled like sex. I was only wearing my top shirt. I stumbled out of bed and joined him, trying to see inside my closet what interested him so much.
"You want to borrow a dress?"
I was sure it was a joke I wasn't getting. I felt pretty certain. I had a reputation for not getting jokes, coming around minutes after everyone else, a big red spot on my forehead to signal my embarrassment. But Brian wasn't laughing, and so, sure that I'd eventually catch on, I directed him to the right end, where the longer pieces hung.
All that I knew of Brian, besides that he loved his two year old daughter, that he was one exam short of a law degree from Iowa, that he wanted to be left alone to what he called his peaceful poverty, besides all these little things I knew about Brian, I knew that I didn't know him. He spilled out details of his life in torrents so profuse that it was impossible to chart him. He was as puzzling to me as his poetry. I could cut pieces of him and paste them to-

gether into a collage of a certain man named Brian, but there wasn't enough geography between us for me to step far enough to see the whole picture.

So, that dress, flowing black lace and cotton that he wore over his combat boots that night: it was a long gown stitched of glamour and romance. It barely fit, stretching tight around Brian's muscular arms. Did he want a purse, I inquired, pretending to be in tune with his madness. Nah, that's gay, he said.

He wanted to go out on the town.

"Wearing that?"

"I just want to see if anyone will say something."

I kidded myself that I sort of understood what he was after. I remembered that my friends had been caught with their race pants down when the boy I kept talking to them about once walked in on us at the coffee shop, surprising us mid-cappuccinos. I had not told them that Brian was black; it hadn't seem relevant, but I remember the tense impact of silence, the strained niceties that exploded to overcome the initial, silent shock of Brian's race. So I went along with Brian, his combat boots and dress, without a question, trying to be the hip, edgy kind of girl he could love.

We strolled on the main square, sat by the fountain across from the lighted coffee shop, gazing at the dressed up gaggles of grad students, fraternity and sorority girls and boys pouring out onto the streets on the way to the many reasonably priced beer-havens of Iowa City. Measures of guitar solos from the live rock bands floated up to us with the drunken yahoos and guffaws of college students ready for summer break. Brian, an Iowa boy from birth, couldn't step three feet in one direction without someone recognizing him, from serving at the diner, from law-school or high-school, or from having a meal conversation interrupted by his third-column advice. People high-fived him, said whatsup, too embarrassed to mention the obvious.

Only a few asked, "What's with the dress, Brian?" and tried to be in on the joke, saying they had worn a dress, too, for a party or for Halloween, speaking with that high-pitched enthusiasm people only adopt when they're embarrassed for you. Then a pride of drunken bullies stalked out of a club, its leader roaring "look at that clown!" as he spotted Brian. I wrapped my arm around Brian's neck and nuzzled him protectively, my hands in his hair; again I was the distraction, the incongruent element of an otherwise simple picture. The drunk's irises literally bobbed inside his beer-moistened eyeballs as he stared at us, a doubt like an ice-pick etching the corners of his down-turned mouth.

I had seen that same look on my face so many times, in the webbed, paint-splotched bathrooms of bars and restaurants I'd frequented with Brian, checking my make-up, my breath, wondering if I'd said something wrong or if there'd been spinach stuck between my teeth. And that's when I got it: I was the dress, too tight, ridiculously girlish, and old fashioned. The joke was on all of us.

Years later I'd remember seeing photographs of Al-Quaeda men posing in lipstick and high heels while embracing semi-automatics, the contrast between their tender femininity and their weapon-clad machismo turning them into fragile things to behold, strange, deadly flowers of humanity. As I read about the artist who collected those photos, who recognized the beauty of the terrorists' violence against their own most delicate desires, I remembered Brian, and the riddles he posed for others to answer about themselves.

I fell in love with a boy, but the boy didn't fall in love with me: what did you expect of a recovering alcoholic and a lonely, serious-minded Italian? When Colin Powell held up his vial of anthrax to an audience of stunned Americans, I was alone in my bedroom, clutching a pillow, and Brian was in Minnesota, trying to sober up. Afghani children were still hungry, and the country was still at war. I had an email from Brian. It said, "I must have mistook dependency for love."

I learned my lesson about spells.

But after a few months, after all the boxes were broken down, and all the books placed on their shelves, I discovered that I'd managed to lose my framed collage of newspaper photographs. I forgot it in the closet of Brian's old apartment, now leased to someone new, someone who denied ever having seen it, someone who may have found it occupying too much space in that back closet, and who might have given it away, or thrown it in the trash for someone else to find, someone else to puzzle over it, someone else to ask, "Who made this?" and wonder.

Strawberry Banana Whole Wheat Pancakes

In Italy there is no real correspondent for pancakes. However, for centuries, Italians have enjoyed a fried variant of a flat doughy treat known as frittelle (fritters). This recipe is for the healthy-minded who still like to indulge a sweet tooth now and again.

1 cup whole wheat flour
1 cup all purpose flour
5 tsp baking powder
1 tsp cinnamon
¼ cup packed brown sugar
½ tsp salt
2 large eggs
2 cups orange juice
2 Tbsp triple Sec
3 tsp vanilla
1 ½ cup chopped fresh strawberries
2 overripe bananas, smashed

Mix all dry ingredients. Add all wet ingredients and banana, stir till just combined with no dry spots. Gently fold in strawberries.

Heat a skillet to medium heat. Dot with olive oil. Pour ¼ cup of batter onto the skillet and cook till bubbles rise and then pop on the surface of the pancake. Flip and cook the other side till lightly browned. Keep warm in a 250 degree oven till all the pancakes are cooked.

Serve with butter, real maple syrup and/or unfiltered honey, and powdered sugar.

Remedy for attracting love into your life:

Find a pretty glass bottle with a cork that fits tightly on it and fill it with dried petals plucked from a blooming rose and some lavender. Fill the bottle with rose water and cork it tightly, whispering your wish for love. Store the bottle in a safe place in your bedroom. It helps the wish to say a novena to St. Helen. To dream of a future husband, on the night of the summer solstice place three fava beans under your pillow: one bean must have been peeled completely of its skin, the second should have its skin removed only halfway and the third should be whole. At night, you will dream the face of your beloved. First thing as you wake up, reach for one of the fava beans under your pillow: the naked bean presages marriage with a poor person; the half peeled bean with a comfortably established person; the whole bean predicts marriage to wealth.

Safe in Your Head

I. Babbo's Religion

My Babbo liked to watch the soccer reports on the state channel. Every Sunday after lunch he sat on the long end of the sectional couch in shorts and wife beater, leaning forward between time outs to hear the reporter rattle out scores of other games, and everyone else in the family had to be quiet during this sacred time.

Mamma eventually came out of the kitchen handling a mop and a bucket of white vinegar. She looked up, saw my Babbo settled on the couch, his thick curly hair sprouting from under his wife beater, and she went back into the kitchen. A moment later, she returned with the buffer.

"You're not going to do that now, are you?"

"Hmmm?"

Babbo watched, with his round eyes unblinking, as Mamma plugged the buffer into the socket near the tv. The roar and whine of the buffer quickly overwhelmed the jingle on the black and white tv and while Babbo waved silently for quiet, Mamma pushed the buffer up and down the living room marble floor until Babbo roared, "Christ, woman, now? Do you have to do that now? Can't you see I'm watching soccer?"

Mamma maneuvered the buffer with one hand, the other waving like a rodeo cowboy on a mechanical bull, shouting even louder, "Soccer! Soccer! Always soccer! *Qui non si vive.*"

This is what Mamma did all day, every day of the week: slosh delicates into a lukewarm, soapy tub; hang shirts and sheets on a clothesline; scrub the grout with a toothbrush; leave the faucet running; shine the door knobs; polish the furniture; spray the window sill; clean the oven; open the windows; dust the plants (don't forget the back of the leaves); fold the clothes; and always, always, always, scrub the stove top with a steel pad. A gleaming house shone all around her, waiting for the cat to vomit on the carpet or for one of us to spill a glass of milk, or drag in mud from the courtyard.

The smell of vinegar wafted through the high-ceiling apartment. The cat, before he ran away, put up brave fights against my mother at least once per week, hissing under the bed, arching his back and cursing in cat language, until she pulled him up by the soft fur on his neck, and dunked him in bathwater, scrubbing him with rosemary shampoo. We could hear his cries through the closed doors for minutes at a time, until the blow drier whooshed. Then he surrendered, exhausted and seduced by the warm blast of air and my mother's brush, too weak to fight off the inevitable, finalizing spray of perfume. (We found him once, days after he ran away the first time, on the lap of a prostitute who lived on the second floor; he was eating canned food and hissing at the huge ragdoll cat on the lounger that was too fat and too comfortable on his recliner to pay our cat any mind. The prostitute's heavy perfume may have inspired feline hope for a soul companion).

Babbo shut off the tv after the soccer report was over, exactly at two.

Mamma was done with the buffer and ready for the vacuum cleaner.

In a preemptive strike, Babbo waved his finger at me: "Don't sit around all day, watching that idiot box. Go outside. Or go do some homework."

Then the door to his studio shut and locked. We could hear him shuffling papers until Mamma, hours later, called "A tavola!"

He was the last to sit at the table, timing his entrances with the grating of the fresh Parmesan cheese. He ate his pasta under Mamma's muttered complaints, "Burrowed in your studio! What am I, the servant? I'm just here to cook and clean, heh?" She bounced a *michetta* on the table, the crunchy, crispy, delicious Milanese version of the dinner roll. Sometimes the roll missed, but sometimes it hit his plate, or a glass of water. Babbo ignored it, his head hunched low, his mouth sucking up the noodles, his lips ringed in tomato sauce and his big round eyes rolling as he threatened with his silent look to slap us if we didn't stop fidgeting, stop playing with our food -- or even if we just considered leaving that slice of liver uneaten.

"But you're eating pasta!"

"You're growing. You need the iron."

"No fair."

"Silence! I'm your father." A hand slapped the table. Glasses rattled.

Mamma shoved her fist under his nose. "Padrone. Padrone."

Babbo liked to shout at the TV. His vocabulary was simple: Goal! or, Ma che cazzo!

Mamma censored his cursing, crying, "Oh! Oh! Vittorio!"

She had the mouth of a port-town Tuscan, therefore, her curses were the most colorful, but only when she was angry. We could be "damned, ugly, rabid assassin mutts," or more modestly "without grace." Our crumpled clothes looked like they'd been "wound tightly up the asshole of a dog." Babbo's secretary was "sausage casing." But a standing ovation for the best curse of all went to my father on Christmas day when we packed the car for a day trip to Torino, and it rained, and the battery died, and the Fiat did what Fiats do: it refused to recharge. So Babbo crashed his fists on the steering wheel and said, "That bastard baby Jesus was born today and he's pissing on me in every color."

"Oh Vittorio!"

In Elementary school, the Italian teacher's favorite writing quiz question was: "Your Father's Job Is:" anticipating unimaginative responses like, a doctor, a dentist, a teacher, and the all-encompassing "ingegnere" or office administrator. The space for the response was never more then three centimeters long. I tried various shortcuts: businessman (Teacher: too vague); salesman (Teacher: what does he sell?); director (Teacher: what or whom does he direct?).

My father's title was "general director of an international consulting firm for the pharmaceutical industry," as exotic as an astronaut without the benefit of the succinctness.

I tried to trick my mother into giving me a simpler answer. "What kind of things does Babbo do when he's at work?"

"Oh, he travels a lot. He goes to France, to England, to Germany, to the United States. He negotiates contracts between pharmaceutical factories and their distributors. He speaks all those languages, your father, and he has know-how in pharmaceutical technology, which is very rare. He has two degrees, one in pharmacy and the other in biology."

No help there. "I need something simple. For example," I shuffled my instructions importantly, "teacher, doctor, farmer..."

"He's General Director of an International Pharmaceutical Consulting Firm."

"Should I write, General?"

"No. Write it down exactly as I told you."

The bile burned holes in my child's stomach when I got the usual red marks indicating points taken off for "bad cursive," accompanied by the comment, "keep to the margins."

Bad grades had to be signed by parents.

Babbo was shouting at the tv when I drummed up the courage to show him. I handed him my assignment and the pen. His big mouth tugged down at the corners.

"What? Don't you know what my job is by now?"

I rolled my eyes as he lamented out loud that in America he'd have made a fortune with all his talents, but we lived in Italy, *il paese di merda*: the country of shit...with a beaurocracy so intricate as to be the butt of all European jokes about hell.

"And they gave you a five? These state-hired morons! Who did they pay to get this job? The government pigs eat from the shoulders of workers like me. They tax us down to our underwear. In America, if you overpay, they send you a refund. A refund, can you imagine? In Italy, if you pay too much, the government will say, 'So we didn't tax you enough!' They'll keep your money and charge you more on top of that for that you had the arrogance to pay them all you owed..."

I nodded. My sense of social class was skewed. We attended private schools but we were poor by comparison to the sons and daughters of other industrialists because Mamma shopped at the cooperative, whereas the other kids sported Fiorucci and Valentino and wore clogs imported from Holland. Our clogs were made in Italy, with good Italian leather because mom, raised by farmers, refused to spend money on what she called *snares for knuckleheads*. For this, and for our slight Tuscan accent that seeped in on our otherwise perfect Milanese talk, we had been proclaimed *terroni*: dirt clods, people made of mud and soil, as if called up by God himself to rise up from farmland.

In fact, we'd reached the apogee of Italian ambition: we owned a three bedroom condominium in downtown Milan, we hired a cleaning lady to help my mother with the ironing, and in addition to owning the two cars, which my father jealously stored in an almost unheard-of gated garage, we drove a company car, a sedan, an Italian Fiat, the model and color changing from week to week according to availability. The cars looked all more or less the same: four doors, cushiony fabric seats, ashy-smelling, and, like all things Italian, neither too luxurious nor too shabby. They often didn't start if we'd had an overnight frost, which was frequent enough during Milan winters. So when it was Babbo's turn to take us to school, my brother, my sister and I would sit quietly with our wool-gloved fingers crossed, huddled together in the tight back seat, hoping the battery would die out before Babbo's determination.

Meanwhile Babbo cussed at Italian cars, Gianni Agnelli, and

the government sellouts who allowed the unions to flip their nose at corporate efficiency by letting them manufacture cars below the standards of the Americans and the French. He alternatively slammed his gloved fist on the steering wheel and worked the starter into a cough, until he'd turn to the backseat, his breath condensing in great puffs of steam, and declare: "Never mind! Today we take the Renault."

When we finally marched to our classrooms on those fog-misted days, an hour late, our necks swaddled in wool, our noses moist with melted frost, the classes were wet and mostly empty.

"They all called in sick," the janitor would mop after our mucky footprints. "But not the Valenza, Amen! What suspense. If the Valenza call in sick, call the ambulance, grab the crucifix, pray to God: it's the end of the world."

Babbo was on the road more often then he was home, but when he got back he had a story and a gift: chocolate pralines from France, a Japanese geisha doll from Tokyo, giant lollypops in rainbow colors, tiny carved Buddha figurines, a stuffed panda the size of a tall toddler. In Mexico, he ate fried worms; in Japan, he ate raw fish; in Thailand, masseuses stomped on his back with their bare feet; in Egypt, a camel stuck its head into his bungalow's window, waking him up with long laps of its tongue; in America everything was extra large, buildings, cars, even frogs, and especially hamburgers. He told us these stories with a special catch in his voice.

But his favorite story of all wasn't a travel story at all. It was the story of Americans who landed during World War II, delivering Italians from starvation with bars of bitter dark chocolate and rusty cans of syrupy fruit. The food fell from the sky, attached to silk parachutes as planes flew overhead, their vivacious roar announcing hope and life. My father was twelve.

He told us that American soldiers had taught him his first words of English. They sent him to fetch water from the wells in the cow pastures. He sometimes ran with buckets dangling from his hands while enemy planes flew overhead and bombs hissed, earth exploding in geysers of soil, turf raining on his head. But they always delivered on their promises, peanut butter, chocolate, American rock and roll records, potato chips, bubble gum, and jokes mumbled in that charming American drawl.

After telling this story again, he grew silent, his green round eyes bulging out and to the side, his thick mouth distended in something not quite a smile, and he'd nod to himself. He had memories, fond enough to cause him to yawn out a wistful sigh. Somehow he'd managed to find a shard of gratitude, even for war.

Then suddenly: "L'Italia e' un paese di merda," (Italy is a country of shit). "Kids, repeat after me," a finger stuck out like an orchestra conductor. "L'Italia e' un paese di merda."

II. Liver Lover

No Babbo at home, no fights. No fights, no faucet running, no soccer game blaring, and no Mamma demanding, "Set the table! What are you, sloths? Did you do your homework yet? Pick up your clothes."

It's cops and robbers time. It's time to throw Laura's doll out the window. It's time to punch Luca in the arm until he gets a bruise. It's time to steal the Barbies and throw them in the toilet and cover them with shaving cream.

Mamma, mamma, mamma, mamma, mamma....

She's sitting on a stool, or crouched near the bath tub, leaning against the sink with a sponge, or a broom, or an article of dirty clothing in hand, shaking her head and moving her lips, caught in the middle of an intense debate in her head.

Mamma, Luca threw my doll out the window.

She's a bitch. She called me a cretin. Then she punched me here, here, look here.

He stole our Barbie dolls.

They wouldn't let me play.

"What? Don't bother me. Can't you see how busy I am?"

Mamma was obsessed with scrubbing an invisible spot behind

the kitchen sink. She bent over it with her teeth gritting and her neck muscles tense, like she was scrubbing nonsense out of our heads, the toothbrush scouring the surface back and forth.

Mamma, is it true that cows make eggs?

(Scrub. Scrub.)

Mamma is it true that Santa Claus said Luca is a bad child? Didn't we call him? Didn't we just call him on the phone, and didn't he say that he wasn't going to bring any presents for Luca?

(Scrub. Scrub.)

Mamma, they keep telling me that cows don't make eggs.

(Scrub.) Hmmm. Hmm?

Mamma is Babbo Santa Claus?

(Scrub. Scrub.) Allora? Leave me alone. You're getting the floor dirty.

But given even just one second of my brother's well-pitched cries, she snapped alive and kicked open the bedroom, closet or bathroom door: wherever Vittoria happened to be hiding in, my sister's fingers already wrapped over Luca's mouth, her voice panicked as she parleyed some kind of truce, ("I'll give you my dessert tonight and tomorrow, and my allowance for two weeks if you shut up right now, a whole two hundred liras per week, eh? What do you say?"), and suddenly sandals, shoes, toys, arms, fingers, raining from everywhere, striking everything, and only the sounds of our "Ouch! But I didn't do it!" and her "Mh! Mh! Don't! Care! Who! Did! What! Mh! Mh!" and the clapping of skin on skin, and the trembling of walls as objects hit them, and the snap of static rising from our hair was our chaotic universe for a good five minutes or more. Mamma didn't care who was right or wrong. She'd beat us all up in fairly meted-out shares until she'd exhausted her strength and was ready to go back to that invisible spot behind the sink that needed scrubbing.

"But what did *I* do?" we screamed at her retreating form, stung more by the injustice than by the red finger streaks on our cheeks.

"I don't know, but I'm sure you deserve it."

Luca, who somehow seemed immune to pain when the whacking came from Mamma, massaged the side of his head with his middle finger, a fool's smirk playing about his mouth, as if he'd just demonstrate the power of the H-Bomb, a power that, yes, could in fact destroy the entire planet several times over, but what potency, hey?

Of the Ten Commandments we learned at Catholic school, Mamma and Babbo were most fond of one, "Thou Shalt Honor Thy Mother and Thy Father."

It was Vittoria's idea to draft a formal retaliatory plan against God's unilateral vision of family harmony.

We sat on Vittoria's bed, each of us armed with pads, pens and pillows, the orange wool coverlet crinkling beneath our crossed legs. Now and again, a pillow flew, usually in Luca's direction. Artillery returned, my hair snapping with static, stood on end.

"Shut up, cretini, we have to finish this. The sibling coalition, hear me."

Vittoria sat up on the bed, tucking her legs beneath her. She was twelve, and almost with breasts. Luca had taken to sneaking up when she was dressing to touch and run, or to snatch her bra and wear it on his head, running around the house in his socks, crying, "Look at my new hat!"

Now he rolled back and forth on my bed, rubbing his face and laughing, pulling the lower lids down from his eyes and making monster sounds.

Vittoria cleared her throat, and began reading:

The Sibling Constitution

1. *Never, under any circumstances, betray your sibling to Mamma and Babbo*
2. *Never confess a sibling's violation of house rules, not under threat of a whooping, nor even in the face of overwhelming evidence;*
3. *When a sibling is punished, the coalition is punished; when a sibling triumphs, the coalition triumphs;*

4. *So that the coalition may take effective preventive action from retaliatory power, all house rules violations must be immediately reported to the head sibling, Vittoria.*

"Why are you the head sibling?" Luca whined.

"Because I'm the oldest." Her hand flew to Luca's face. Luca parried swiftly with his arm and rolled from the bed to the carpet. He looked at me like one who is hatching a plan: he'd inherited my Babbo's bulging round green eyes but also Mamma's cunning.

Vittoria was in what her doctors called "the idiot stage." I wasn't sure exactly what that meant, but according to Vittoria, it meant that she liked to touch people, often, and rudely, as when she chased me around to pinch and rub my ass because she knew how I'd just pitch a fit over it, or when she'd rub against Mamma's back, purring and wiggling her eyebrow, making exaggerated pleasure sounds.

Luca rubbed his head and complained, "I want to be head sibling. If you don't let me be head sibling I'm telling Mamma."

"You cry baby. You shouldn't even be playing with girls."

"Exactly. I'm a boy. Therefore I command. And also, Mamma says I'm the most responsible."

Vittoria snorted. "You can't even draw. You break our Barbies because you don't even know how to play, isn't it so, Laura?"

It seemed somehow I'd managed to persuade both Luca and Vittoria that my judgment was the most reasonable.

Mamma, when she caught me trying to stop Luca from crying, or getting Vittoria to apologize to him, screwed her mouth like during one of those silent debates she held with herself, and said, "L'Aque chiete, eh? L'Aque chiete rovinano i pointi. Always scheming like a cat that plays dead. Know what they say about calm waters? Calm waters ruin bridges. You're trouble. I know."

But Babbo was more likely to observe me with his big, round eyes, and after a while he might pronounce, "My daughter, The Wisdom Keeper." He nodded, silently, like a capo Mafioso approving of an unspoken contract.

"Right, Laura?" Vittoria insisted, pinching Luca's butt.

I thoughtfully noted that we liked to dress our Barbies and Kens while Luca preferred to dismember them and hide the limbs in the linen closet. We liked to color the flowers in our coloring books according to coherent schemes. Luca preferred to zigzag wild lines across the page. We preferred to dress up the cat in dolls' clothes. He preferred to sling it until it spun around and clawed his cheek on its way down. "All this, seems to me," I pronounced, "Indisputable evidence that you're immature and too much a boy."

Luca rose from the bed with his mouth open in an expression I knew rather well: I had the power to make him stop crying with a little persuasion, but he always observed, even in the most bitter of his sniveling, that I ended up taking Vittoria's side in the long run, on every dispute.

"But it's not fair!" His cry was high pitched enough to send Vittoria scurrying to shut the door of the hallway. "Vittoria is the one who's always getting us in trouble because she's always taking cookies from the pantry!" His finger pointed accusingly.

I rubbed my chin, and noted, "That is true!"

"But you have that hair bands thing," said Vittoria. "And that's just abnormal."

Some kids collect marbles, toy soldiers, even cars. Luca had a hair band fetish. He had whole bags of them, which he hid in his bedroom in a secret place under his toy drawer. We suspected he snuck into our bathroom to steal the colors he did not own, and then refused to relinquish a single one even on our worst hair emergencies. How he had hair bands in the first place was a mystery to us, but Mamma insisted that she bought them for him at the supermarket, a thing that we found as perverted as Luca's penchant for ripping Barbie's legs and arms, an action which he always preceded with an enthusiastic, Look! Look!, like a surgeon about to demonstrate a tumor extraction.

"Listen," Vittoria said, breaking the impasse. "If you want to stay, I'll let you stay on condition that you become our slithering slave. That is, whatever I say, you do it, but you have to do it by slithering on your stomach. Every time you do something by slithering on your stomach, you earn a point. With enough points, you may even be promoted to kneeling slave."

Luca slammed his way around the apartment, crying, "Girls are so mean! I hate giiiiirls." He then marched into the kitchen and petitioned Mamma for a brother.

Vittoria and I adjourned the meeting and congratulated each other on a firing well executed. We expected the usual backlash: dismembered dolls, disappearing hair bands, our piggy banks violated. We were prepared and devised stratagems to thwart him: a box of shoes on the half opened door to alert us of his comings and goings; secret hiding places in Mom's bathroom, strings tied to the cabinets where we kept our bigger dolls.

Days went by and Luca was unusually quiet, retreating to his Mickey Mouse comic books and playing alone with his cars. The shoebox fell on Mamma's head when she called us for dinner, one night. Luca secretly smirked behind her while she massaged her head and demanded, "Do you think it's funny to throw shoes at your mother? Sloths!"

But it wasn't until weeks later, one night at dinner, that we first glimpsed the ruthlessness of Luca's plan. We heard our mother's usual call: "Vittoria, Laura, a tavola," which was our hint that it was time to put the plates on the table and wait another hour while Babbo may or may not come home in time. But when we got to the blue-tiled kitchen, the plates were already set on the table, and Luca was sitting in his usual chair, against the wall, spying us from an uplifted fork he held up to his nose.

Attached to the fork was a cube of repulsive, slimy, greasy, stinky liver.

"Ewww, liver," Vittoria complained.

"I don't want it I don't want it I don't want it I'm not hungry," I began my slow litany. Luca on the other hand, stuffed a cube of pre-cut liver in his mouth and chewed.

"Liver is good for your skin and your eyes," he began. "It is full of iron and vitamins and small children need to eat liver in order to grow up healthy."

His last words fell on our shocked silence.

Mamma sang from the stove, "That's right, Luca. What a good boy. You see what an intelligent boy your brother is?"

"Mmmmh, mmmh," said Luca from his throne. "Liver is delicious."

He stuffed another cube in his mouth and chewed with his mouth open.

"That's right," said Mamma with her lips pursed, enchanted enough to wean her attention away from the polishing of the stove burners, even as she was still preparing my father's meal of spaghetti Bolognese and a veal cutlet with capers. She bent down to Luca, grasping his large head with her wet hands, and still clutching a sponge that now tickled Luca's neck as she deposited a torrent of kisses on his head, saying, "My son is such a smart, handsome boy. He's such a good little boy. Not like you girls. Sloths! Good for nothing. Luca helped me to set the table today."

We began to glimpse the genius of Luca's allegiance with the dark side. Luca's legs dangled from the high chair. He swung them back and forth as he ate until his feet kicked our shins.

"Ouch!" I complained, rubbing my knee with as much tragedy as could crack my voice.

"Don't tease your brother," Mamma warned.

"But he kicked me!"

A sponge hit me square between the eye, its splattering sound making Luca cough up his half chewed up cube of liver. I stared wide-eyed at my strategic brother. Mamma's aim was infallible. With his liver eating, Luca had bought himself the most powerful artillery available to child-kind.

Vittoria slung a liver slice at his cheek.

"Ouha, Mammahhhh! They always hurt mehhhh!" Luca cried, not bothering to wipe away the streak of grease and sautéed onion that stuck to his cheek.

"Why-did-you-do-that," Mamma began, her hand already

raised to strike. "He was sitting there peacefully, eating his liver…"

Luca raised the crying a decibel or two.

"Disgraziata," Mamma cried, her lips already folded around her teeth, and that was a bad sign, a sign that at any moment now, she would seize whatever was within reach and throw it before she even ascertained if her grenade was a glass vase or an old shoe. She was dangerous that way. Her unfortunate choice, this time, was an ice cube.

It flew in a perfect trajectory with a flick of her delicate wrist, and landed square in Vittoria's open and excuse-filled mouth, whereby it ricocheted off her front teeth and sliced a tiny wound on her upper lip, inflicting a tear that, to Mamma's unfortunate and belated regret, would never again heal right. While Vittoria hollered, holding on to her new bruise to squeeze as much guilt out of Mamma as a child can squeeze from a scar-giving parent, I skulked to my room, shutting the door behind me on the noise. But Mamma was not long coming after me: "What are you up to? You don't fool me with that innocent face. You know what the proverb says? Calm waters ruin bridges! L'acque chiete rovinano i ponti."

III. TU VO'FA' L'AMERICANO

The color animated cartoon Heidi, about a Swiss girl from the mountains ran a total of an unimaginable fifty-two episodes, straining the attention of prepubescent Italian children beyond hitherto untested endurance. It started at 4:30 exactly. There was just enough time for Mamma to pick us up at school and drop us off in the condominium complex's gardens downstairs for our usual game of tag on skates. After approximately two and a half laps and a good jostling and wrestle, the kid with the lisp held up his hand and pointed to his wrist watch, and we knew it was time to race upstairs to our fourth floor apartment—after calling the elevator and pressing every button just to upset the only kid with a color television, who lived in the penthouse, of course.

We knew to ring the doorbell like a maniac so Mamma might

hear it through the vacuuming, and then we'd bolt through the door, wash hands in the guest bathroom, brew a cup of tea, steal a slice or two of salami from the refrigerator and sit down to the fifteen minute summary of the previous episode, which, of course, was always interrupted by various commercials on Nutella, pneumatic tires, and laundry detergent. Then we could enjoy fifteen minute of the rosy-cheeked midget-sized Swiss girl and her much prettier paraplegic friend Clara doing things that were generally uninteresting except for the last two minutes' cliffhanger, which was invariably followed by yet another slew of commercials, which we also, invariably, endured. Still, we somehow managed to be surprised when all that followed the three minute commercial break were tantalizing snippets of what we could expect in the next episode.

But five minutes to episode forty one, Mamma answered the door at the first ring, and as we catapulted ourselves through the door, throwing the skates into the closet and crowding around the sink, shouting, "Mamma, turn on channel two!" Mamma waited for us in the kitchen, seated by the television, where instead of the Heidi show we were assaulted by a breathless rattle from a special edition of the telegiornale: Aldo Moro went home to his family in the trunk of a Renault 6, perforated by ten bullets, and very much dead.

"Your Babbo and I have a surprise for you," Mamma said.

I clapped my hands together and gasped. The last time Mamma had spoken those words, it was to announce that she and Babbo had invested their savings in a summer beach cottage on the Sardinian coast.

In the least, I was expecting a new kitten.

"We are moving to America," Mamma said.

Vittoria whined a high-pitched "Oh, no! How could you do this to me."

"Why," I asked.

"Because your father thinks it's best," Mamma said, but my question had been directed at Vittoria. From what I could remember of my fifth grade geography lessons, America was home to Hollywood, the Mississippi river, Tom Sawyer, cowboys and Indians, the Rocky Mountains, the Grand Canyon, and Disney Land. All in all, America sounded like a swell place to me.

"It's only temporary," Mamma assured us. "Just enough time for all of you to learn English and enrich your career prospects."

Mamma had called it a surprise, but it was, in fact, the apogee of my father's long-term strategy, the secret he had been saving for that night at the dinner table, his fingers twined together, his lips tainted purple with the wine he'd drank. His usual orotund voice turned pregnant with meaning over the hushed telegiornale and the frenzied images of the black and white camera covering the usual spoils and destruction in the wake of the latest demonstration. Screaming young people ran under the police's rubber bullets, posters with the communist pick and scythe abandoned on sidewalks littered with broken glass.

"It is necessary," he began. "Aldo Moro, the ex prime minister, was killed. The police are idiots. The whole government is an idiot. It is all one big corrupted, infected system. It pains me to say, but Italy has turned into a third world country. They kidnapped another business executive and shot him in the back, and this after the family paid the ransom. At the Pierrell, all the executives have been told to hire personal security. Starting tomorrow, Federico will take you to school in the Pierrell's car. It is dangerous and all of us must be home before dark. In America, instead of working from seven in the morning to nine at night," he said, reaching for Mamma's fidgeting hand in an unusual and somewhat insincere display of affection, "I can get home at five thirty, and the family can vacation at Disney World. Imagine Disney World, kids."

The promise of Disney had Vittoria stuff a ball of soft bread in her mouth which she had carved out from deep the inside of the loaf of bread she'd been torturing, and Mamma spoke the first and only complaint she voiced at the dinner table: "Oh, Vittoria! Bread will make you fat."

Then Babbo proceeded to finalize the decision he said he'd taken on behalf of the whole family and instructed us to select the toys and clothes we could absolutely never do without. We would be throwing away the rest.

"Will we be gone forever?" Vittoria asked.

"We'll see," said Babbo.

Although Mamma had remained quiet and pleasant all throughout dinner, and although she'd praised Babbo's business savvy and even gaped at the six figure salary he expected to earn, her front crumbled deep into the night, when her anxious whispers dotted by the occasional, "Shhh! The kids will wake up!" rose steadily as the hours wore on. Eventually the whispers broke into shouts, then heavy accusations, then the thumping and stomping of feet, and the trembling of walls as objects flew and smashed and Babbo's voice declared, "Enough! I need sleep, woman. I have to work in the morning."

But Mamma's violations of the Geneva Convention didn't advance her cause much, so her next strategy was to leave notes around the house, in Babbo's wallet, in his sock drawer, in the glove compartment of the car. We'd find them taped to the phone receiver and prominently exposed on the refrigerator or the doorknob to Babbo's studio. All of them said the same thing she hollered at him the minute he walked in through the door:

Admit it: you think that you're Napoleon!!!

The fact that Babbo's birthday fell on the same day as the famed Corsican dictator persuaded her that her propaganda war was, if not effective, at least justified.

But Babbo ignored the notes.

"I make the decisions," he'd punctuate with a fist crashing at the dinner table. "The family stays together."

There came the day when Babbo's warnings became more than just kitchen commentary on the news of the day. True enough, Mamma was cautious venturing beyond the school-home -supermarket track in her Fiat 500, but there were sales all over Piazza Del Duomo, irresistible with those mannequins wearing cashmere sweaters and Gucci skirts reduced 30%, 40%, even 50% off the original price. The mannequins tempted Mamma in dreams, painted smiles promising daughters spit-polished for Sunday mass and school functions, and so even her one-eyed blindness and the threat of a demonstration wasn't enough to keep her from a good bargain. Lured with the promise of a new gabardine pants and leather loafers, Vittoria agreed to ride on the passenger seat of the 500, the little white FIAT bumping over the trolley's tracks as it approached the historical Duomo district. The two of them braved the icy slush of melted snow, past the pigeon-shit speckled piazza and the Gothic cathedral and into the lighted domes of the Galleria, unflinching from the tempting smell of warm pastry and fresh espresso wafting from the many lighted cafes and marching straight to the bargain-bin SALDI of Ferragamo out-of-season clothing.

A solicitous salesman immediately offered them water, a Fanta, a cup of coffee. Mamma sat on a cushioned chair while Vittoria tried on the attendant's selection of velvet pants with matching vests and long skirts, stabbing pins into the fabric at the hemline and waist, and crying, "Signora, at the price I sell it, it's a great bargain anyhow. But if you buy the skirt and the sweater to go along with it, I give you a purse, and a cashmere scarf to match it. And maybe a little discount, too." A hand waved side to side.

But at the climax of these negotiations, when Mamma made to get up from the plush chair, grabbing for her purse on the floor with a flashy jingle of her gold bracelets and whining, "Well, it's not such a great bargain, eh? But I suppose it's good quality-" it was then that the overhead speaker music cut off in mid warble, and the roar of people crying out in panic pushed through the spaces between Mamma and Vittoria like an uncouth farmer-assassin.

The attendant slapped a hand over her mouth, crying, "Oh, mio Dio!" and Mamma turned her head in time to see the owner hook the shutters with a metal bar and block their exit with metal. The shutters groaned, casting a dark shadow onto the floor. The mall outside responded with the panic shuffle of a dispersing crowd, more glass shattered, explosions and loud, popping sounds followed by wisps of smoke and the distant siren of a police car.

"Wait a minute," Mamma cried. "What about us? How do we get out?"

It seemed to her at that moment that her fear was punctuated with the unmistakable crash of glass breaking. A store alarm whined and the rush of feet and panicked voices seemed to multiply.

Within moments Vittoria could see flames from the cinch, as the shutters could not be shut all the way from the inside.

The way Vittoria later described it, Mamma covered the twelve or fifteen meters from the mirrored sitting area to the front shutters in two leaps, and the next thing Vittoria discerned with clarity was Mamma clinging to the shutter's square handles, pulling with gritted teeth and a reddening face not unlike Luca's when he tried to expel a particularly large turd. She released a slew of Tuscan insults at the owner, including the usual: Twisted. Deficient. Assassin dog. She gave up on the heavy shutters and waived her closed fist at the flabbergasted man instead, crying, "I refuse to let you keep me prisoner here. If we ever get out, I will sue you out of your grandmother's dentures."

"This is kidnapping!" an encouraged middle aged woman complained, who had stayed put observing Mamma's struggle with the shutters.

"You have no right to keep us in here!" another shrieked.

The owner lifted his hands to the sky, pleaded with God on the insensibility of women, slapped his hands over his face and once again looked to the low ceiling of his store, until a thin, pale-faced girl in a cotton dress pointed out, "There's a back exit, signore."

They filed out like thieves, with their heads low and their high heels tucked under their arms, and entered a scene of smoke and rubble. Molotov cocktails crashed and burst to flames under cars, while young, long-haired activists with leathers shoes and cardigans smashed display windows with crowbars. One would have expected them to be quoting Calvino instead. Vittoria and Mamma ran through shards of blown glass, over littered sidewalks. Policemen in helmets and plastic shields were firing tear gas on mobs. For once, Mamma was glad she hadn't found parking anywhere near the mall. Her Fiat cinquecento had a ticket on the windshield. Vittoria and Mamma got away with a little soot on their foreheads, a broken shoe heel, a dent in the cinquecento from a thrown glass bottle, and a breathless story to tell.

But that was the start of the bad season. Days later, the bomb threats began, right before lunch break at school, and we'd file out from our classrooms to stand too dangerously close to the squat cement building of our elitist private school, while firemen searched in vain for bombs that didn't materialize, and while the Pirelli factory workers next door, who were on strike, eyed us with interest and odd satisfaction. Why weren't we supporting the strike? They wanted to know.

"They're only children," A brave teacher ventured. "For God's sake, leave the children out of it."

"We have children, too," a worker said, waving a fat finger in the air like a music conductor.

An hour later we were home to tea and cookies well before our usual time, and a frantic Mamma was on the phone with our nonna, saying, "I know, Mamma. I don't really want to go, but Vittorio, Vittorio decided. What can I do?"

IV. BELLA CIAO

Babbo had developed his passion for travel during his military service in Italy, but Mamma had never left her hometown of Piombino until she married, and then only to be traumatized by a temporary residence in Denmark, where my father had been transferred to open a new affiliate. There, she had spent her first married year pregnant, freezing, and gesticulating in sign language at the local market for her groceries.

Still clumsy in the kitchen, my mother once managed to buy an eel at the fisher's market. The fisherman who sold the eel wrapped it in newspaper and tried to explain to her how to clean it, but besides a few terse exchanges in bad English, my mother nodded, flashed her famous smile, blinked her pretty blue eyes, and walked away with the wet newspaper package tucked under her arm, understanding not a thing.

At home, she cut up the eel in pieces and filled the sink with water to soak the eel, but no sooner had the cut up pieces touched the cold water that they shot up from the sink and bounced around the kitchen in a post-mortem exclamation caused by the eel's electric charge. Mamma chased after the pieces with a hammer, smashing around after the demonized eel, believing she was the focus of vengeance of a dead underwater serpent. And that is the image I hold for my mother when I recall how she tried to adjust to life as a newly minted New York immigrant.

One event dominated the mind-set and emotions that ruled Mamma throughout her life: it was the memory of one chilly morning in April at a funeral home, a crowd pressing before her father's grave, already festooned with red ribbons and kerchiefs, and a long line of mourners offering condolences to her weeping mother. Her father's head, wrapped in swaths of bandages, smiled lifelessly through the serene art of the embalmer. She recalls buckling under the heat of her anger, incapable of understanding the invasion on hers and her mother's grief. It was 1951, dawn of the cold war, froth on the first swells of Communist witch-hunts, and her father had been a Resistance fighter, an anti-fascist organizer whose trade was in the steel industries.

During the war, because of his politics, he'd been embedded with the Germans in Russia. When Italy's government changed allegiances, solidifying a sly pact with the United States, there were no official orders reaching the foreign divisions that Italy was no longer allied with Germany, but the zing of bullets echoing from the wrong end of the front sent the message clearly enough to my grandfather: the marriage between Italy and Germany had never been a match made in heaven, but in Russia, all attempts at pretenses dropped with the subzero temperatures and the harsh cracking voices of Germans executing pleading and confused Italian soldiers.

My grandfather survived by hiding under an overturned Russian tank. Later he walked his way back through the steppes, until the frostbites and hunger nearly killed him. But he wore the red bandanna of the resistance, and the party card tucked in the folds of his torn uniform earned him the pity of two elderly farmers who felt moved enough by his frostbites and the scabs on his head to nurse him back to health.

The year my grandfather died, the local paper had printed an incendiary anonymous editorial:

> Only six years after the dictatorship of Mussolini, and already we see our fiercely earned democracy wrested from our hands. It is imperative that the dispersed forces of the anti-fascist resistance re-organize immediately to protect the freedom that our brothers and sister earned with their blood.

The editorial followed the controversial dismissal of the elected Mayor of Piombino, a close family friend to my grandfather, who had dared to plead with a Minister during a formal inauguration of new machinery to leave steel production to the reconstruction of Italy, and not to the making of weapons for the impending Korean war. The Italian Minister, whose former ties with Mussolini's government had somehow evaded post-war justice, traveled across the country flanked by armed bodyguards and US officials of the Marshall Plan, visiting steel mills and giving speeches, and throwing childish fits when citizens pleaded for peace. When the mayor of Piombino made his, the Minister tried at first to wrest the microphone from his hands. The crowd hooted and booed him. The US Official looked on in agitation, a translator inadequately drumming whispers in his ear. Shortly later, the Minister turned on his heels in a move too reminiscent of a Nazi parade and returned to the awaiting helicopter.

And then, the mayor was fired. And then, there came the editorial. And then, the workers of the steel mill at Magona set up a strike. Shortly later, a rash of sympathy strikes covered the entire Italian peninsula. The question my Mamma never dared to ask herself: What was her father doing at three in the morning, traveling a deserted road on the back of a friend's Vespa? Why wasn't he in his bed, his arms thrown around my grandmother, his body limp with needed rest before his long work hours at the mill the next day?

The road that my grandfather and his comrade traveled that early morning after the meeting was a popular commuter route, well paved, but empty in those early hours. I imagine the spit of light trembling ahead of them on the asphalt, the narrow curves around the rocky hills, the steep slopes flanking the road, rising up on their left and dipping into the Mediterranean to their right, the low-pitched whine of the Vespa overtaking the cooler hush of the waves below. Then, just past the rocky outcrop of a narrow curve, there, an unexpected shimmering, an object ahead of them on the wide, dark road, and panic, the frenzied wobble, the sputtering motor, popping tires and crunched gravel, their own shouts cracking over the wild soughing of the wind.

My grandfather, they say, was bucked with amazing force, and when he fell on the side of the road, the luck that had carried him safely through years of anti-Fascist riots and battles on the Russian front abandoned him suddenly like a cheap whore, like Mussolini's government on a losing Germany: he hit his head on what was described to my eleven year old Mamma as "a very pointed rock." It happened to shatter the lower edge of his skull plate and to skewer his medulla oblongata.

I would, one day in a very distant future, browse through the ubiquitous Internet to discover that this area of the brain is described in sniper manuals as "the apricot," the preferred body target in situations when the intended victim is at a significant distance or on the move. While the formal investigations never could explain the delay, nor how the roadblock sawhorse ended up on that street, the uncles and the aunts nonetheless dismissed the accident as a terrible tragedy, and after the well-attended wake, the event never again attracted public attention.

My mother, on the other hand, remembers one peculiar early morning when women in dark coats knocked on the door, took my grandmother to the kitchen, sat her down, boiled some water for coffee and lit cigarettes. They told my grandmother that there had been an accident, that her husband was wounded.

Minutes later, Mamma was a shadow in a place of whispers and nudges, involuntarily exposed to the most brutal revelation: "He's dead. Cold as marble, already."

When my mother was eleven, her blue eyes and elaborate beehive coifs earned her runner-up in the local pageant, and already she was counting on a future spent before ticking film cameras, surrounded by the flashlights of the paparazzi and the autograph pads of eager fans.

When my mother was fifteen, she came home too often to an empty house and knew already where her mother could be found: at the cemetery, on the consecrated burial grounds between the scatter of tombstones and clods of dirt, fuming in the cold as she observed, with steady fascination, grave diggers exhuming old cadavers to make room for the freshly deceased.

At forty, my mother often shot out of bed with teeth clenched and cold sweats, rushing to Luca's room, pushing her hands against his face in the dark, patting the length of his body, certain, in spite of the reassurances of her senses, that she had lost him on the dock of a cargo ship, like her great grandmother warned her in her dream.

At forty-one she opened letters addressed to Vittoria and listened on the other phone, announcing her presence only when she could no longer hold back, and shrieking: "My daughter is not going anywhere after dark, you hear? Who are you? What kind of girl goes out at night without a chaperon?"

At forty-three she stormed into our closets, overturning shoeboxes, digging for secrets in the pockets of our coats, and in our underwear drawer.

V. SAFE IN YOUR HEAD

Vittoria met Claudio at Italian school that first year of our exile. He was a gangly, dark eyed soft-spoken boy who dressed in button-down sweaters and wore a Jewish kippah on his short-shaven head, having recently converted to Judaism in an unexpected inversion to the more familiar reactionary teenage angst. Vittoria had turned into a pretty girl, with languid amber eyes, an easy laughter and a contagious smile. Both strangers, both fragile stalks in the jungle of New York, both virgins and both believers of true romance, these two newly minted expatriates made their journey from friendship to first love between ringing class bells and lunch recesses.

"Invite him over for tea," Mamma mentioned casually one afternoon, noticing Vittoria's persistence in mentioning his name. The way Mamma held her head high, her blue eyes turned into fissures, her mouth tensed into a fake smile should have warned Vittoria, veteran of Mamma's wily traps, that Mamma had caught on. But Vittoria's heart was in sugar, steeped deep and encrusted with the certainty of happiness that only a fool can trust.

"Tomorrow? Is tomorrow after school ok?"

Claudio, dressed up in his good shirt, dark sweater, and good leather shoes. He even wore a tie for the occasion. But still could not be persuaded to do away with the kippah. A good middle class Italian boy, he was polite to Mamma, shook her hand and spoke to her in the appropriate third person. He refused snacks vigorously, as was expected, but ceded at the peak of Mamma's insistence. He complimented Mamma on the beauty of her clean and orderly house. He sat next to Vittoria, but kept his hands on the table where Mamma could see them, although he was sure to rumple Luca's hair with brotherly affection. We were sitting around the kitchen table, with our afternoon tea and our tray of cookies.

Mamma's eyes kept bouncing from Claudio's teacup to his fingers to the top of his head. She'd hover over the sound of her words before she spoke them, with her blue eyes squinting a little, dimples forming at the corners with her wrinkles.

"But Claudio, aren't your parents Catholic?"

"Sure they are," said Claudio, fidgeting with a half eaten cookie and assuming a seriousness that didn't match the shadow of a premature mustache on his teenage upper lip.

"You have some Jewish relatives?" Mamma asked, her chin pushing forward already.

Claudio shook his head and looked for recourse in a sip of his cooling tea.

"So why the hat?"

"It's called a Kippah," said he, importantly. "Men in the Jewish faith have to cover their heads."

"Ah," said Mamma. Her mouth hung open for seconds after the exclamation came out. Her chin moved forward in a half nod, but her lips tugged down in a frown. "Are you crazy, or what?"

"A little," said Claudio laughing. "I am undergoing conversion and studying about the faith. If I want to make the final decision I will have to be circumcised."

It was clear that this last bit of information held interest for Luca, who straightened suddenly in his seat and said, "That's when they cut off the tip of your dick, right?"

Vittoria exploded in her tea. Claudio politely pretended not to notice that some of it had sprayed his good suit.

Mamma, holding her fingers bunched up and waving her hand, attempted a mumbled, "I don't get it."

"I work for a Jewish man," said he, finally. "It's not so much for the faith; it's for the people. I admire the suffering of the Jewish people," he finalized, in a phrase that sounded a little too rehearsed. He shrugged off the rest of his explanation by belatedly removing the kippah from his head and squeezing it in the palm of his hands. Mamma flattened her lips against her teeth and swallowed her unnecessary reply: we knew that her uncle had been tortured by the fascists, that her father had died in the name of idealism, that even Babbo's people had suffered nightly raids, slashed mattresses, shattered furnishings and long beatings from those who would accept no political demur. She came from a long line of atheists and Catholic orthodox, and she thought she knew something about suffering.

"Well, then," she said, and made a gesture of her hands that seemed to suggest grandiose things. Her lips thinned against her teeth. "It's getting kind of late, eh?" She fingered her watch on her wrist while fixing her eyes on the kitchen clock instead. Claudio caught the hint and got up.

"I thank you for having me over," he said, squeezing her hand.

"I forbid you from associating with that crazy Neapolitan," Mamma told Vittoria no sooner had the front door shut on Claudio's back.

"But why!"

Mamma usually didn't brook contradictions, but that night her reply came in the form of a tight fist that knocked against Vittoria's head several times in quick successions. "Because I-said-so!!!"

Vittoria and Claudio's romance took on the romantic appeal of a Shakespearean tragedy, sighs exchanged with Vittoria's "But my mamma won't let me!"

The two met at recess in the hallway of the school. They met in the vestibule in the morning, their umbrellas dripping from the rain. Sometimes, the Principal would nudge me into a corner at lunch: "Your sister feeling ok?"

With the instinct of a loyal sister, I'd shake my head gravely.

"Is that why we haven't seen her since homeroom?"

"Very sick," I'd act out, holding my stomach. "She had to go home."

"Hmm." The Principal fingered her chin. I secretly prayed she wouldn't call home.

In the afternoon, I often sat by myself in the favored ice cream parlor, sucking on an empty straw for drips and drops of chocolate milkshake, watching over Vittoria's school bags and those of Claudio as they walked around the city block to sigh and ponder their doomed romance. I survived the monotony by dreaming secret romances, wondering if I, who didn't have a sensuous mouth, or a loud and vivacious temper, would ever find somebody willing to put up with all the restrictive peculiarities of my mother and father. My middle name in school was Ugly. What kind of guy would meet me in the morning with a rainy umbrella and carry me off to the wonders of Manhattan on a school day?

One day, before I got home from school, Vittoria got impatient and left me a note on my pillow: Mamma thinks I'm with you. Come down to the lobby and wait for me there. Claudio and I are out by the playground.

Mamma, who had been shopping, returned home before I did. She spotted Vittoria and Claudio as she was vacuuming; she looked out the window and saw them walking down the cobbled street that cut through the condominium complex. They were holding hands. At some point, Claudio slipped his arms around Vittoria's waist and pulled her close to him in a kiss. Mamma watched Vittoria and Claudio kiss, and kiss, and kiss. She tried to open the window, but safety precautions in New York prevented her from obtaining more than a little slit of an opening. She shouted out, *Vih, Vih, Vittoria!* the vacuum cleaner still roaring, but from the ninth floor, only the neighbors heard.

It was easy enough to imagine what Mamma saw: a convention of black-clad women whispering at the window as they would have had she lived in her home town: *the Valenza's daughter is kissing a Jewish boy*, the women whispered in Mamma's head. The frowns, the upturned eyebrows, the covert smiles exchanged at her expense. But more than that, I imagine her thinking of the story she often told when denying us permission to a party, or an afternoon at the movie theater: she'd been five in the post-war, starving, and picking up a piece of sausage that a boy, who was happily skipping on the sidewalk just a few steps ahead of her, had carelessly dropped. It took but a few seconds for her to pounce on the meat, but by the time she held it in her spindly fingers the morsel of sausage was already covered with ants, writhing with the busy insects as if alive. She popped it in her mouth all the same.

And this memory dictated something spiny and bitter: that being careless with one's reputation in this flammable world of Jew-haters, this world were safety was as fragile as the thickness of glass, this was not something Mamma could tolerate, least of all of her own children. Vittoria would not be like her Mamma, woken in the middle of the night by women in long coats, carrying smoky breaths and news of death. She would not marry a troublemaker who left her bed at night to go to secret meetings.

I'd rung the doorbell several times. I could hear the vacuum cleaner whooshing, yet no one was answering the door. I used my keys to get in. I saw that Mamma had her head pushed against the window, her knuckles beating fast against the glass.

"Vittoria! Vih…! Vittoria!" she called out.

When Mamma turned away from the window, she was startled. For a moment, she was screaming without sound.

"It's me, Mamma, it's me," I tried to reassure her.

"You stupid? Why don't you ring the doorbell before you come in? You think it's funny to frighten me like that?" Her fists bounced from my arms. "Where is your sister?"

It didn't take a genius to figure out that Sister was out with Boyfriend, but my loyalty, of course, was always to the coalition. *Never, under any circumstances, betray your brethren.*

I'm sure Luca would have argued that the only one who ever came out winning from coalition rules was Vittoria. I could have just said, I don't know where she is. I haven't seen her since this morning at school — but I couldn't do that to her. Luca might have remained pragmatic, estimating ratios between the number of times he bore through a whooping on account of her and the number of times he actually deserved one, but I could still remember my sister waking up to my whimpers after I'd wet my bed when I was three; I could still remember her ushering me to the bathroom, coaxing me to a quick bath, changing the sheets of my bed, and finding me a clean pajama, all the while reassuring me that she would not tell Mamma. I could still remember even the times that I'd wake up crying from the rheumatic pains I've suffered since age three, my feet and legs feeling like I had giant pin needles stuck through them. Vittoria patiently massaged my feet and tucked them into a set of socks that she'd warmed up first on the radiator.

"She was with me just now. We were down at the playground, reading, but she forgot something there. Her math book, I think. She just went back to get it."

I felt my head snap back with the blow. And I didn't need to look in the bathroom mirror to know that there was a handprint on my face where I was feeling the heat rise.

"Liar! You and your sister are like the Mafia! It's the Camorra! *Io no sacciu. Cosa nostra.* Your sister is a whore and you, you play the mafiosa. Like the proverb says: l'acque quiete rovinano i ponti."

She hit me with her flat hands; then she rubbed her knuckles on the top of my head. It went on for a while. If I covered myself with my arms she'd slip off her sandal and hit me with that. What was she hitting? Even at twelve, I knew it wasn't me. She was hitting my father, for moving us to America, and making her lose a daughter to a boy who might not be able to protect her if politics got crazy. She was hitting Americans for the unrestrained sexuality of a culture that she could not understand, for a freedom that frightened her as much as it made her jealous. All those things my Mamma was shedding through the palms of her hands and through her knuckles on my scalp.

By the time my sister got home, Mamma had vented most of her rage on me, and was too physically exhausted for a second round with Vittoria. There was a lecture, a scolding, and a warning, and she was off the hook.

Had we ever discussed this incident beyond the facts, I'm sure Luca would have said I deserved it. He was never a big believer in our solidarity. The older he grew, the more he preferred to be by himself. When Babbo's best friend had driven us to the airport that one last day in our home country, it was Luca he spoke to, a finger raised to his nose, as though he knew the first betrayal of Italian values would come from him: "Don't be a traitor to your people now," he said. "Don't you come back here some years from now and say, I'm American, doing things like an American. Remember where you came from. Remember who your real family is."

What had that man known that we did not? What had his friendship with our Babbo, the American devotee, taught him about our brother Luca's future?

Luca didn't know who his family was. To him, we were the crazy people he tried to hide from his American friends, the ones he embarrassingly denied kinship to when he partook in making fun of us louder than his friends. To Vittoria and I, Luca was incomprehensible. Americans were incomprehensible. They fussed so much about their flag and country, and they were ready to kick their sisters and talk back to their mothers. What was country to us? The Italian Republic had had fifty-two governments in fifty years of its existence. It had betrayed us with Mussolini, with fascism, with communist socialism, with Brigate Rosse, with inflation, with unemployment, with educational reform that strove to uneducated everyone. The only thing worth anything to us was family. Just that. So what if your family was crazy? To us, the family was the only country, albeit a country under constant riot. In our disunity, we were unified. The family was together: that is all that mattered.

Even so, by the time I turned fourteen, the screaming between Mamma and Babbo was constant. I'd often wake to hear it in the middle of the night, my mother's accusations bursting out between sobs, "Sono una disgrazziata; sono dannata." I am a disgraced woman; I am damned. It wasn't the words that created the tragedy, but the passion with which she believed in them. Peace in our home, once assured, at least, when Babbo was away, became ever more rare. Sealed up in loneliness, separated from her family and friends by an ocean, failing to understand the culture her kids were growing up in and even the language they spoke, Mamma was turning morose, her lighter side waning by degrees as the years wore on.

We did not know that her depression was curable. We lived with the certainty that madness was the romantic privilege of those who had suffered. Besides, my mother was suspicious of doctors, called them butchers and assassins: perhaps because fascist doctors, under the auspices of medical research, had tortured and murdered Jews, communists, rebels, anyone who threatened the regime, and Mamma had relatives to attest to this fact; or perhaps because she came from a family of farmers who cured themselves of hay fever by laying shivering under bales of horse's hay and drinking quinine. On the few occasions we managed to take her to a doctor, the endeavor turned out to be self-defeating since she refused to take the medication the doctor had prescribed.

So we lived with it. She could be a kind and lovable mother for weeks on end, but volatile and explosive in a moment gone wrong. We agreed she could carry things too far, but then again, this was the woman who would iron table napkins and bras, the woman who would wash the underside of plant leaves and spray a newly shampooed cat with perfume. If she could be that demanding of cats and plants, was it really surprising that we failed her ambitions every day? We tip-toed around her, trying to read her moods with our emotional barometers, and ducked when the windstorm arrived.

Then, one morning, I woke up hearing Mamma thumping her fists on a door.

"Vittorio! Get out of there. I was there first. Get out," she shouted.

I ventured out of my bedroom and into the master bedroom to find my mother in her bathrobe, banging her closed fists against the bathroom door.

"I'll be out in a second," Babbo called out cheerfully. His tennis bag was propped near the door. He'd probably snuck in for a quick shower before his Sunday match.

Mamma rapped hard on the door. "I was first!"

"I'll be out in a second." The faucet turned on.

"What's going on?" I asked cautiously. "Why can't you just use my bathroom?"

"Noh!" Mamma hissed through her teeth: "I've been scrubbing that tub clean for an hour. I wanted to take a bath. I just stepped out to get my bathrobe, and he scuttled in. He *knew* I wanted to take a bath; I'd left the water running. Now by the time he gets out, the towels will be wet, the floor will be wet, and there will be hair in the drain, *his* hair. He has no respect for me." Her voice had reached a shrill. She couldn't even talk anymore. She made a strange gesture with her hands; then she marched to the kitchen. I could hear her rummaging through cabinets and drawers. Only Luca went after her.

"My God, she's got a hammer!" He cried from downstairs.

I locked myself into my room and stood by the door with my hand on the knob, hearing Mamma stomp back to her bedroom. Luca was still chronicling for us:

"Oh, my God, what is she going to do? Oh, my God, she's going to *use that hammer.* Oh, God, I can't believe...Mamma. Holy shit!"

We heard the thump, the cracking noise of wood splitting.

I dared open the door and peak outside. I ventured to the hallway, where Vittoria and I exchanged a meaningful glance. Mamma was in the master bedroom, hammer in hand, hitting away at the bathroom door. The door was falling apart in chunks, and Babbo, visible through the widening hole, held a comb to his part, watching the hammering through the reflection in the mirror, paralyzed in stupor. We all suspected that Mamma was perfectly capable of throwing that hammer at him with the same force she was employing to break down the bathroom door. When the hole became as wide as the circumference of two large melons, Mamma brandished the hammer.

"There," she shouted. "There is your damned bathroom. Are you happy now?"

And when she finally dropped the hammer, it was Babbo's turn to rage.

"Crazy, stupid woman. You belong in an asylum. You're a lunatic. I'm going to have you committed. Kids? You all saw it. Your mother is insane."

By then, Babbo had us removed to suburbia, enrolling us each in a modestly reputable public school and posing another obstacle to our struggle with adaptation. No more Italian school for us: now we had to parade our weirdness to the social judgment of bored suburban teenagers, who hated us for the way we ate cafeteria bagels like they were sandwiches and pooh-poohed us for washing our hair only every other day. Mamma was probably hit hardest with the change: at least in New York City, she could stroll down the street and window shop, distract herself with the glitz and life of the Big Apple. Here in suburbia, she only had the flowers and the trees, and a big car in the garage to reminder her that her driving was inadequate for the unfamiliar highway system. My mother every day resembled more and more those placid characters in Hollywood horror movies whose niceness and good will unexpectedly turns to eerie cruelty.

One afternoon, Mr. Anderson, the English as a Second Language teacher, showed up at the door unannounced. He was a strange looking man, with coke-bottle glasses and jeans that billowed at the knee and rose a half an inch too high for his long legs. He wore worn blue sneakers with laces he clearly never bothered to wash. He was fond of a brown button-down cardigan, which he wore over his collared shirts.

"I just wanted to stop by," said Mr. Anderson, "to tell you how wonderful your children are, Ms. Valenza."

I spied Mr. Anderson from behind Mamma, feeling my heart thump against my breastbones: poor Mr. Anderson didn't know how rude he seemed to my mother. And when Mamma said, "Please, Mr. Anderson, come in," he accepted, not understanding the Italian rite of propriety that would have demanded he refuse her invitation. And when Mamma said, "Laura, why didn't you tell me that Mr. Anderson was coming?" he did not understand that no matter what he said to reassure her that I didn't know, she would never believe me.

"May I make you some hot chocolate?" she offered.

I felt my cheeks burn. Mr. Anderson fixed me with his cow-brown eyes, offering his version of an innocent look. "Ms. Valenza, what a nice lady you are. I would love some chocolate, thank you."

I saw my mother's lips tighten and felt embarrassed for Mr. Anderson, too American to understand he was placing unreasonable demands on my mother's hospitality rhetoric. But my mother went to the kitchen and left me to entertain Mr. Anderson while she whipped up her cioccolata calda: pudding mix diluted with whole milk.

"What are you doing here?" I hissed at him.

During lunch break at school I had made the mistake of asking Mr. Anderson for a pass out of gym class. Instead of simply refusing me, as any of the normal teachers would have, he instead demanded to know why I wanted to skip. I gave him the standard teenage reply: "Forget it, ok? Forget I asked." And because he insisted, "Jeez, Mr. Anderson, I said forget it, ok?"

But Mr. Anderson had some ambitions about himself that no one else shared with him. He wanted to know. "I know you wouldn't ask if it wasn't for a good reason, but I want you to feel comfortable here. We're a family here."

The two Japanese girls and the one Peruvian who were scheduled for ESL that period where all silently staring at me, their foreign eyes blinking blank, their language barrier sparing them embarrassment.

"Come," Mr. Anderson said, jingling the massive key-ring attached to his belt, and he pointed to his supply closet. Once, the kid we all referred to as Carlos the Columbian had yelled, "Fuck you, Mr. Anderson, I ain't going into your gay closet," thereafter putting a rest to the notion that ESL students were better behaved then regular Americans. But Mr. Anderson still pushed us to that closet when he wanted to have a private talk. Once or twice, he'd managed to get me to follow him in there, and today we both sat on an old desk in the dark with the dust and the photocopy paper and the boxes of chalk and highlighters.

He inched closer to me, asking, "What's wrong?" fishing for an excuse to wrap his arm around me, breathing his bacon breath on my cheek until finally, as much to get him off my back as anything, I told him: "Some girls at gymn, they push me around in the locker room. They stick their dirty menstruation pads on my locker. They call me Ugly, and Moose and all sorts of names."

For some reason, I began to cry. I think it was just Mr. Anderson and his big jiggling key ring that pushed me against the drama.

Now he was in my living room, causing problems and making Mamma cook.

"Why are you here?" I hissed at him.

"I want to talk to your mother about you," he said, beaming an idiotic smile. "Laura is a wonderful student," he said to my mother, when she came back with the hot chocolate in her good china. Mr Anderson slurped too loud and smacked his lips. "She's very smart, you know Ms. Valenza," he concluded with chocolate stained teeth.

"Oh yes," said Mamma, her hands rising to give fluff to her words. "She's smart yes. And Luca. Luca is very smart. My son, Luca, you know him."

"Yes, Luca is smart," said Mr Anderson. Then, squinting his astigmatism my way and winking, he added, "But I think Laura is smarter."

"Hmm," Mamma said noncommittally. She made a motion with her chin as she looked at me. "Well Mr. Anderson, it was so nice of you to come."

"You're a very nice lady, Ms. Valenza," said Mr. Anderson. "I wanted to meet you because your daughters say you are such a strict and rigid mother. But I can see now that you're a very nice lady." He beamed at me, his pallid face crinkling with glee. "Your mother is very nice, Laura!"

When he was gone, Mamma chased me to the bathroom where I was trying to escape. "Say it! Luca is smarter than you are. You stupid girl. Luca is smarter than you!" Each denial on my part was accompanied by a hefty slap in the face from her. ("Hit her back," one friend suggested, after the fact. It's as if I'd turned to an American in need of paper towels and said to her: "Use the flag." I gawked, silently wishing away my friend's blasphemy).

Mamma was bent on dividing and conquering and she knew how to do it well. On occasion, Mamma would go to spend the afternoon at the mall. She'd come back with a bag. She'd call us to the family room and throw the bag on the couch.

Vittoria had a tendency to soft curves, while I was bony and angular, my hipbones poking through my skin.

"Aren't you ashamed of how fat you've become?" Mamma said, looking at Vittoria. "I bought these jeans for your sister. I would've gotten you a pair, but you'd have looked like a sausage in them. It's time for you to lose weight. I can't stand it any longer."

My sister grew up with the absurd notion that I was prettier than she when every boyfriend and every romance should have assured her of the opposite. On the other hand, Vittoria's success with boys was my personal Achilles' heel. At fifteen, when most of my American schoolmates had at least one or two romances to reminisce upon, all I had to sport were a series of nicknames. Big Nose, Flat Tits, and Pimple Face were the three most popular ones.

But there was one boy who was not ashamed to be seen around me: Tony, the second chair bass clarinet player, the new arrival from Italy, his Neapolitan jolliness preventing his prejudice against the most unpopular girl in school. As far as Tony was concerned, I was a paisana, and one of only three in a school of several thousands equipped to understand his clever puns in Italian.

He was short and muscular, with a round face that was always alight with smiles. I do not think that Tony's interest in me went much beyond my suitability as an audience; nonetheless, he seemed willing to overlook what Americans could not forgive, even the fact that Mamma would forbid me from going to parties or from wearing makeup. For a few happy months, Tony and I sat next to each other in band, blowing out our ghastly marches into our unwieldy bass clarinets with more breath and enthusiasm than talent. We smiled at each other in between spit-cleaning breaks, exploring the depth of our immigrant bond as we suggestively slid felt rags through the shaft of our instruments: it was Tony's mission to update me on all the jokes I had missed since my last visit to Italy, and my fixation to make even the lamest of his updates appear hilarious.

"And did you hear the one about the soccer player at the supermarket?" Before I could answer he went on: "A wordy supermarket manager recognizes a famous soccer player who was sold to the Brazil team. The manager shakes the player's hand and says, Everyone in Brazil is either a soccer player or a hooker, isn't it so?' The very insulted soccer star replies, 'How dare you? My wife is Brazilian!' And the manager says, 'Great! What team does she play for?'"

When it was the tenth grade's turn to do a history drama sketch, Brillo showed up with a baseball cap turned backwards and an old leather baseball glove on his hand. He strutted in, his moon-shaped face illuminated by his enormous smile. "Hi!" he waved wide, "I'm Tony, and you're not."

To clarify, he rubbed his kinky hair, so tight and springy that he did resemble the pot-scouring pad. He sang the ditty for the commercial.

The American boys cheered, "Brillohhh!!" There were hoots and whistles, and that was just his getting started. By the time his presentation ended, the room crashed with applause.

I realized that my time as Brillo's exclusive audience was ticking to an end.

"Great presentation," I sidled up to him after class.

He swung around and, pointing a finger at my chest, he shot:

"What's green and flies over Poland?"

"Do you want to come over for tea and cookies, or something?"

"Peterpansky!" Tony burst. His thick eyebrows crossed over his eyes. "What?"

"Cookies," I said. Then I remembered and opened my mouth and pushed out the most persuasive laughter I could muster: "Ha ha ha, Peterpansky. You're so funny, Tony. You make me pee."

He shrugged, waved at a passing gaggle of hooting Americans. "Hey!"

"Brillo!" they howled back. And "who's that?" Whistles.

I was flattered.

Brillo...Tony walked with his head pushed forward, a bounce to his step. His shoulders kept working up and down, as though he were trying to shake off a kink in his muscles. "Yeah, I guess I could come over for cookies."

I crossed my fingers and held my breath: months of letting my knee casually rest against Tony's when we sat together in band, months of my laughing at every stupid joke that spilled from his constantly moving mouth...I was sure Tony knew how I felt about him. My heart seemed to be rising into my lungs. I swallowed. What would mom think when she opened the door and saw Tony? I could at least count on Mamma's sense of propriety from making a scene in front of a guest. I could handle her third degree later. Then there was the fact that Tony was Neapolitan, and Mamma... well...

I bounced next to Tony, with my cheerleading: "That joke about Poland, do you have any other jokes?"

He did! He shot the punch lines out before I might steal the thunderbolt from him, but the smiles he detonated made up for the sophistication that lacked in his delivery.

When we got home, it wasn't Mamma in the kitchen, setting out cookies on a tray and boiling water, but Vittoria. "Hey Tony," she waved without looking at us. She was wearing her thick wool sweater and ripped jeans. Tony knew Vittoria from band, too. For some reason I could not fathom, as soon as he saw her he quieted. The smile on his lips spread like a crack.

"What kind of tea would you like?" she asked him.

"We only have one kind," I said. "Lipton."

"Lipton!" Tony laughed, like it was one of his jokes.

"We have chamomile, too," said Vittoria.

"Jesus," said Brillo, bending back like he'd been shot. "I thought you might have something like Earl Grey or English Breakfast."

"We're not that kind of tea drinker," said Vittoria. She sat between me and him.

"What's green and flies over Poland?" he asked.

"Peterpansky!" I said.

Vittoria squeezed her eyes nearly shut, her mouth open as she let out a hiss of laughter.

Not long after that, I sat back behind my cold cup of Lipton to witness the tickling and giggling, the ice-in-the-t-shirt reuse, the rolling around on the floor with whooping screams that invariably led to V. and Brillo's first romantic embrace, followed by the kiss, complete with tongue and teeth.

I saw their mouths meet, but by then it was anti-climactic.

A few days after the event, one of the more competent counselors noticed my moping around the hallways, retracting to silence. They called Mamma to a conference.

"I know why you are slacking off," she declared when she returned, her face so close to mine I could smell that she'd started smoking again. "You're whoring around with boys, like your sister. Like they say, calm waters bring down bridges!"

On a Saturday morning, I woke up to the usual cacophony of the family fights:

"If Luca can go to Sean's party, I can go out with Tony tonight."

I lifted myself from bed and crept to the door of my bedroom.

"You can't stop me!" were the first words I registered when I saw Vittoria and Babbo, standing in the hall within inches of each other. Babbo's face was flush. When he spoke his voice came out in bursts.

"Vit-to-ria! Vit-to-ria! You-know-what's-going-to-hap-pen-if-you-cross -me." He'd already lifted his hand to strike her. Mamma was the one usually doing all the screaming and beating. When Babbo got involved, it had us shaking in our shoes. He seldom hit us, and never hard, but he was the Babbo, often spoken of in third person. The Babbo had to be obeyed. His threat loomed larger than his real self.

"You can't stop me," Vittoria shouted.

"Don't you say another word or I'll hit you," the Babbo threatened.

V. took a step back and Babbo fatally assumed he was winning.

She said, "If you hit me, I'm going to call the police."

Mamma screamed, Vittoriohhh! Vittoriahhhh! Pleeeease! "

I knew V. well enough to know that Tony's black Camaro was parked out on the street, and that he would be there to put her back together, regardless of the result of this confrontation. Whatever was coming out of V. was more his than hers, but her voice was eerily calm, as though the inevitability of her situation had finally dawned on her.

"If you hit me, I'm going to call the police," Vittoria repeated.

Babbo tried to gauge her seriousness from her face, but he had never been around us long enough to know us, had never bothered asking the right questions, never thought to study our responses, our reactions, our words, our wishes, our way of expression. He had never even imagined, really, caring for us in any form other than paying: paying for our school, paying for our clothes, paying for our car and gasoline consumption, paying for our vacations, our skis, our movie tickets. For as good as paying was to us, for as certain as we all were that it was lucky that he did, for as much as we knew that many dads didn't even do half that much for their children, paying was certainly not the same as knowing. And that was our Babbo, very good at paying, very bad at knowing.

His was more of a stroke than it was a hit. I'd never seen him hit so gently. Perhaps he felt that V. would take pity on his not knowing, and allow him to preserve his authority and pride. He was wrong.

V. called the police.

"Child abuse," she said to the officer, on the telephone.

"Child abuse," she repeated to the officers, at the door.

Mamma was crying. "*Madonnina*, what shame!" She pleaded with the police officer: "Child abuse? I've never hit her in my life." She pleaded with my sister: "Are you crazy? Your poor father. All we've done for you." She pleaded with me and my brother: "Luca and Laura, tell your sister she's crazy."

"How old are you?" Asked the police officer to my just-turned-eighteen sister. "Don't you have another place to stay? At least for tonight?"

V. ran to her room. She packed a small bag. I don't know what she took. I didn't see her leave. Mamma's hands kept going from her cheeks, to her hair.

This was nothing more than a coup d'etat. Vittoria was striking out on her own. She was dumping family and coalition, starting up on a new road with Tony. I couldn't believe it. I felt like Columbus when the Catholic Kings imprisoned him. After all that loot! I went to my room and from my window I watched the patrol car pull away, my sister in the back seat. V. had lit the dynamite and then ducked for safety. We had all been exposed for what we were: not a family, just selfish, crazy, and destructive people. Our pieces were strewn about with the rubble of her scattered clothes.

Babbo confronted me shortly after the patrol car had pulled out: "From now on," he began, finger raised, "you're to be home from school at exactly three thirty. Not one minute later. That's enough time for you to walk home from school. Otherwise, God help you. And if I catch you talking on the phone with anyone, God help you..."

I had my forehead pressed against the window so he would not see me crying. I missed my sister. I wanted her back. I wanted the illusion of unity back.

Then it was Mamma's turn to barrel into my room.

"Do you think your sister was right?" She hit me before I could reply. "Dare to hit me back," she shouted, her hands coming down hard on my head. "Dare to call the police." Her hits kept falling on my face and everywhere my arms could not cover me. Once again, I was Mamma's punching bag.

I endured the beating through the righteousness of my innocence. But my passivity was the devil's advocate. I was an accomplice in my sister's abdication. Had I believed V. was not coming back, I might have survived the moment like I had survived a thousand other whoopings, in honor of the triumph of freedom, of the siblings' victory over parental despotism, but V. had betrayed us to the outside world, to Tony, to the American police, only to leave me behind to fix things for her, so she could come back in a few days, bouncing with victory, gloating with secret smiles, taking up her role in our exposed fakery of a family.

I found myself dialing Tony's telephone number within a few hours of Mamma's beating. Tony didn't want to put V. on the line. He knew what it was about.

"Please come back, V. Please come home."

"But why," she asked me. "Are they hurting you?"

I sobbed on the phone without answering. I couldn't say who was hurting me, or for what reason.

But after I hung up, I went to the family room, where the television played a seventies family comedy, its music and humor infusing the otherwise quiet room with normalcy. Mamma and Babbo sat erect next to each other on the couch. I took my space in the loveseat at a corner from them. We didn't speak: anger is exhausting, cumbersome, like an overstuffed suitcase without wheels. It was much easier for us to let the quiet speak truce.

When the door clicked open hours later, I knew it was Vittoria tiptoeing up the stairs. A blast of wind ushered in the sounds of flushing rain and the refracting trajectory of Tony's Camaro's headlights. Then it slammed shut, and Vittoria's footsteps fell heavy above us, making the ceiling vibrate. Upstairs, a door slammed, and then another.

Years later, this would be the birth of an accusing refrain, an undying dirge to the dissolution of our distilled absolut of sisterly faithfulness: I should have snuck away from the family room. I should have rejoined Vittoria upstairs right away, to hear all about her adventures with the police and her short-lived escape with Tony. I should have thanked her for coming back, for sparing me from becoming the sole target of Mamma and Babbo's experiments in immigrant parenting.

"Now Mom and Dad will never change, and it's your fault," she accused. Her lips, as she sang the first tentative lyrics of the song of our dead friendship, were poised in the threat of swallowing a gulp of ethyl alcohol. "It's your fault that Mom and Dad will never change. You should have let me be."

"Then why did you come back?"

She shrugged. Her squinting eyes giving away her bluff, as she carefully worded: "Is alcohol poison enough to kill a person? If I drink this whole bottle, do you think I will die?"

"I doubt it," I said. "I'm sure it will give you a bad headache, though."

She tilted the bottle, her mouth half open, her pink tongue still red with Tony's love, and her shiny eyes trained on me.

"So, you're going to kill yourself, huh?" The tone in my voice gave away my skepticism and she lowered the bottle from her lips. She seemed surprised, challenged, even, by my indifference.

"Why did you guilt me into coming back," she said, twisting the cap back onto the bottle. "You don't even care if I'm here or not."

I shrugged, not knowing exactly that I did want her back. I wished she'd showed some spine. Instead, she'd only proved to me that she, too, was only counterfeit American, not maverick enough to stand up to her own revolutions.

"It's your fault," she declared. "Tony said it. If you go back, Vittoria, your mom and dad will never change. He was right. You see what you did? Now we're stuck with this life."

In years to come, that would be her most bitter complaint against me, and the alibi against all the things in life she was sure she could have accomplished, had it not been for me. *Because of you, Laura.... I did it because of you...*

It's a reassuring mantra, one that I wish I could adopt to imagine what our lives might have been like if instead of running away from the carnival of an outlived insurgence we had stayed put and never thought to question who we were. But we get to make only one phone call from the prison of linear time. On that first day of our entrance to the New World, braving the lines of Immigration with our worldly possessions stuffed in old suitcases trailing behind us, if we could have projected ourselves into the future, we probably would have never chosen the things that we became.

Twenty-three years after we crossed the ocean, we would know our mistake with absolute certainty: the one phone call wasted on a busy line. We witnessed the destruction of our last bastion of hope, instead, when our illusion of a safe, impregnable America implode with the steel and brick of The World Trade Center. Each of us, then, sitting alone in a living room or a kitchen, in South Florida, in Iowa City, and in upstate New York, felt at first connected by one eerie flash of deja vu: the lead pipes in the hands of a mob of syndicate workers, the shades drawn down at school, the faces of our teachers blanched and tense as they told us "Bambini! Silenzio! Don't speak a word;" the Molotov cocktails crashing through window shops and landing in a blaze on the asphalt; Aldo Moro on the news, his physiognomy of hope forever immortalized in a stale, black and white photograph…I want to imagine that my Babbo and Mamma saw something, too: the inevitability of history, maybe; the sense that time is one large fishbowl with recycled water, our reflections in the glass tagging after us, haunting us like ghosts. In some odd sense, I think it might have given them comfort.

But that night when Vittoria came back to rescue me, abandoning her Tony to his black Camaro, her handsome blue prince left behind for her mission to protect me, I sank into the leather recliner, my hands gripping the armrest, my eyes fixed on the moving images on screen: the silvery happiness of the moving picture, so joyfully and heartbreakingly American, felt close enough to be mine.

Crostini Toscani

Liver crostini are typical for the Tuscan region, where liver dishes spice the diet of many living in the countryside. They can be served alone as appetizers or with broth as a first course. Many Italian recipes are simply not hard and fast. This is such a recipe. The base is organ meats, oil, and a basic soffritto. After that, let your imagination soar. Mushrooms, caviar, and walnuts are a simple additions, for instance.

1 tsp saffron
2 tbsp butter
1 tbsp olive oil
6 fresh sage leaves, chopped
2 slices of pancetta, chopped
2 shallots, minced
½ stalk celery, minced
3 baby carrots, minced
1 tbsp capers
2 tbsp fresh black olives, chopped
1 tsp pine nuts
8 chicken livers, cleaned
6 anchovy filets
1/3 cup dry white wine
1/3 cup vin santo
½ cup low salt chicken broth
Juice of one lemon
½ tsp lemon peel
I loaf crusty Italian style bread or baguette.
olive oil

Gently warm saffron threads in a covered pot with the wine and broth till the saffron aroma fills the house.

Cut bread into slices. Brush both sides of bread with olive oil and place in a 350 degree oven. Toast for 15 minutes. Remove from heat, let cool.

Add butter, olive oil, sage leaves, pancetta, shallots, celery, carrots, capers, olives, and pine nuts to a cold sauté pan. Heat to sauté. When vegetables are soft, add chicken livers and anchovies. Heat for about 3 minutes till livers are browned all over. Remove all the solids from the pan with a slotted spoon, place on a cutting board and finely chop. Return solids to pan, add wines, broth, and lemon juice. Cook to reduce liquids, but the end result should be moist, not dry. Serve warm over the toasted bread.

Note: There are those who do not like their bread so crusty. Many families will serve their crostini with a bowl of broth handy, for dipping.

Option: Chicken hearts may also be added to this recipe.

Remedy to heal relationships with friends and relatives:

The horns of the snail bring strife among relatives and friends, but eating snails on the evening of the summer solstice in the company of someone dear will bring peace and harmony to one's whole family that everyone will enjoy all year long.

Acknowledgments

I owe the completion of these linked stories to many people and organizations who encouraged me, supported me, provided advice, and assisted me in so many ways that these few words of thanks can hardly define the gratitude I feel towards them all.

First of all, I am awed by the formidable insights and patience of my readers, first and foremost Susan Newman, who read innumerable versions of each story and endless variations of the full manuscript, and also Tina Whittle, Barbara Bottner, Maryanne Sthal, Will McIntosh, and my earliest readers, Les Standiford and Jill McCorkle.

I also want to thank my sister Valeria for helping me with some of the details of Italy and World War II, and my parents, for the family stories that inspired the project and for the details of an Italy now lost to time. A owe a special debt of loving gratitude to my grandmother Liliana whose stories told to me when I was a child ingrained themselves so vividly in my imagination that they nagged at me from the subconscious for decades until I let them out through many of these stories.

Also for their editorial insights, many thanks to Laura Davis for her indefatigable patience, and to Katrina Murphy for her sharp proofreading. My appreciation goes out to the early believers who published these stories in their magazines when they were still tremulous newborns. Also to Lynne Barrett and Dan Wakefield for their spot-on advice on the business of writing and for their patience with my many questions and moments of insecurities, and Mitchell Kaplan and Tom DeMarchi for access to literary venues that enabled me to commingle with so many talented minds.

I also offer my most enthusiastic gratitude to the Sewanee Writers Conference for the gift of a Dawkins Fellowship that enabled me to enjoy two weeks of writers bliss, one of the most rewarding moments of my career, and to the Hambidge Artist Colony, where I completed my work surrounded by gorgeous nature and supported by gifted residents, hospitable staff, and one amazing cook. My fondness for these places is no small matter and I thank those who made it possible for me to attend. Many blessings.

I would be remiss if I didn't also mention the support of all my colleagues at Georgia Southern University, but particularly Eric Nelson, Sonya Huber, Martha Pennington and the late and very much missed Peter Christopher. Your support and encouragement has been a beacon in the darkness. Because you believed I could do it, I kept doing it.

I thank Kimberly Verhines for picking my story out of the many eminently publishable manuscripts submitted to the press.

I thank my many spiritual teachers for giving me the strength the practical tools to believe in myself and persevere, in spite of the overwhelming challenges and the discouraging setbacks, and Bhagavan and Amma for rescuing me from the brink of quitting.

And most of all, I thank my husband Joel, my most tenacious fan, my indefatigable reader, my editor, my personal support system, my inspiration. Without you, none of this would be possible.

Note: all recipes are original and developed by Joel Caplan of Savannah's Cafe Gelatohhh.All remedies are gleaned and adapted from popular Italian sayings and traditions.

About the Author

Laura Valeri was born in the port town of Piombino in the region of Tuscany in Italy, but she lived in various cities in the United States since she was twelve years old. She now resides in Savannah, GA, with her husband Joel Caplan. In addition to Safe in Your Head, she is also author of The Kind of Things Saints Do an Iowa/John Simmons Award winner, and winner of the Binghamton University John Gardner Award. Her work appears in numerous journals and magazines, online and in print. She is Associate Professor of Creative Writing specializing in fiction at Georgia Southern University.